Stealing *It*

Also by Rachel Robinson

All The Way Under

The Real SEAL Series

The Forgotten SEAL

The Playboy SEAL

The Destined SEAL

Stealing It

BRONZE BAY SEAL
Book Three

INTERNATIONAL BESTSELLING AUTHOR
RACHEL ROBINSON

LN
P

Stealing It
Kindle Edition

Love N. Books Press
An Imprint of Wolfpack Publishing
1707 E. Diana Street
Tampa, FL 33610

www.lovenbookspress.com

Stealing It was originally self-published in 2018 by Rachel Robison.

Edited by My Brother's Editor

Paperback ISBN 979-8-89567-669-1
Ebook ISBN 979-8-89567-668-4

For my mom. The strongest single mom I'll ever know.
You are fierce. Brave. Resilient.

Stealing *It*

Prologue

MAGNOLIA

Present Day

THE DROLL SCRATCH of the old-fashioned radio trips, and in that rapid silence, I hear a low voice—a murmur. Seconds later the music returns, a poppy song I danced to anytime I heard it riding in the back seat of the car as a child. Smiling as I sing along, I take the dusting cloth and run it over the tapered chair leg, taking care not to push down too hard. I scored the entire dining set at an antique auction for a steal, but restoring it and getting it ready to sell in my antique shop has taken over all my free time. I never spend this long on my finds, reserving the majority of my working hours for running my online store. People will buy almost anything from the past. All it takes is a tiny bit of nostalgia, and someone, somewhere, is all over it. It's my job to decide what holds the *it* factor with a mere glance. I'm good at it. Rather, I've honed my skill to decide what matters over the course of my life. Perhaps it's because by offering someone a cherished memory I'm erasing some of my own. The ones I wish I never had in the first place.

The song ends and a new one begins after the DJ announces a benefit motorcycle ride for charity this upcoming weekend. The low voice I heard minutes ago grows louder, and while it's not unlike Kendall to chat loudly on the phone to her plethora of friends, I can tell she's upset. Call it mother's intuition, or maybe it's the fact that she's seventeen and angry. When I was a young teenager, I wasn't angry, I was pregnant with her, and scared out of my ever-loving mind. I married her father straight out of high school, and we made it fifteen years before he had an affair with a younger woman. Which is ironic if you understand that the younger *woman*, Pamela, is only a few years older than I was when I got pregnant with our daughter.

Pamela is a stunning brunette who did books for our family HVAC company. We hired her straight out of high school and taught her everything she needed to know to do her job well. Eventually, she did more than accounting well, and Paul did *her* any chance he could get.

Kendall has been irate since the divorce, and she has every right to be. She is the one who found them, in our formal dining room, naked and billowing all over each other. The therapist says my daughter is getting over the incident. Sometimes, when she's busy being a teenager, I think maybe he's right. Other times Kendall looks haunted, her eyes gaunt and her demeanor so withdrawn I never want to leave her in a room by herself. Pamela's age combined with her father's betrayal has left harrowing scars inside her heart and mind. The thought forces a shudder in spite of the tepid heat surrounding me.

Reaching over, I switch off the air conditioning unit blowing in the window and hop off the stool I've been perched on for the past three hours. Rubbing my sore hands together, I sigh heavily. The stifling Bronze Bay, Florida, heat has soaked into my little garage full of treasures, and it's time to check back into the real world, a place that only recently became a location I want to be. After the divorce, I was a scorned woman, but now, I have met a man. A beautiful, confident man who is my polar opposite in almost every way. His self-confidence has rubbed off on me in so many facets. When he tells me I can do something, I believe him. When he says something, it's truth. Good or bad. Building that trust again gives me wings, opening me to a kind of love I never dreamed of having. Kendall is my life. I fully intended to see her off to college and maybe then worry about myself and my love life. Maybe.

One thing remains true. Aidan loves me with a furious passion I've never experienced. Not because he has to or because he's bound to me, he does it because he wants to. He respects me. Aidan makes me feel like my life wasn't derailed, halted, and put on a back burner, but that all my hardships were leading me to something more. He is a man made for more. Made for battle. Made for loving. A soft passion wrapped in a steely package that marks him as gorgeous by anyone's standards.

Butterflies invade my stomach, flapping around in the agony of the knowledge that he's busy training out of town this weekend, and I won't get to see him again until Tuesday. Won't be able to taste his lips or see that devious smile. A grin that sealed my fate the very first night I met him.

The tight pink dress is markedly shorter than anything I've worn in the past decade. This is a date. The first one I have been on in a very long time. I preach to my teenager about being confident in her own skin, never changing for anyone, and yet I can't help but feel like I'm playing pretend. I feel like a fraud. I tug down the hemline as I peer into Bobby's Bar, squinting through the dirty windows scoured by years of salt water and sand. My friend assured me that using this app to get a date was safe in our small town, but I'm uneasy. My daughter is also part of the reason I'm here tonight meeting the handsome stranger who messaged me after we matched. I have to move on, or at least outwardly portray moving on if I'm telling her to forgive her father and move on with her own life. With confidence and poise. Most importantly move on with a forgiving heart.

The things parents will do for their children know no bounds.

I wipe my forehead because the sheen of sweat appeared almost immediately after I got out of my friend Jenny's car. She's going to the beach behind the bar. She's my backup in case I have a panic attack or the guy is awful, and for general support, as this night was born out of her persuading. I rub my hands down the sides of my dress, swallow down the lump in my throat, and swing open the door. The old, jangling bells that thwack against the glass cause a few people to look my way and stare a little longer than I'm used to. I smile at the vaguely familiar faces and nod at the bartender behind the bar when he flicks his gaze up and down my body in greeting.

The young guy slinging drinks tips his head to the opposite side of the bar. Of course he knows why I'm here and who I'm here for. The whole bar knows.

My head swims as I inhale deeply. I let my gaze travel the distance and fall on a man who can only be my intended date. He's wearing a black shirt like he said in his last message, and he stands out among the Bronze Bay regulars. "Here4thePics" looks just as perfect in real life as he does in the photos on his profile, maybe even a little larger than life. I shift in my heels and try to gather my wits as I make my way to him, dodging casual conversation by keeping my face aimed toward the ground until I end up at the empty stool at the very end of the beat-up bar top.

I hold out my hand. "Magnolia Sager," I say, my voice trembling. "You must be…my date. Aidan?"

He looks at me, a cursory glance up at my face, training his eyes directly on mine. "A handshake, Maggie?" he replies, looking at my hand and then back at my face. "I don't shake hands on dates." He turns his head, and I let my arm drop down by my side, my heart pounding out a horrific warning. He is bad news. I feel it in my blood.

"Magnolia," I counter. "It's not Maggie."

His face is even more stunning in person. I know it's all about symmetry. I remember reading about attraction when I was speed-reading self-help books before I filed for divorce. I'm attracted to his symmetry. That's it. His lips are wide and pink. His jaw is square and dimpled, and his eyes, which have to be perfectly aligned because I fail to admit the symmetry chapter can be wrong, are a bewitching hazel color. Green on the outer ring and brown toward the center around his pupil.

While I'm busy fighting with myself internally, Aidan stands to his full height of somewhere in the clouds and leans down, pecking my cheek. "I'm Aidan Mixx, and it's a pleasure to meet you. We're past handshaking, Magnolia. You're here with me." He palms his chest, a chest that I can tell is sculpted through the thin material of his T-shirt. He extends a hand to the stool next to him and grabs my hand. "Will you have a drink with me?"

I forget to breathe. Most particularly, what the hell I'm doing here and how to react when a man is giving me attention like this. Clearing my throat, I sit, adjusting my dress. Aidan watches, I can see his eyes scouring my body in my peripheral vision. "A drink or two is what we agreed to, right?" I say, trying to play it like I do this all the time.

"We agreed to a lot more than that," Aidan croons, drawing my gaze to his. I see an entire night play out before my eyes, and it is a carnal pleasure of a magnitude I have no idea how to tackle. "Didn't we?" he asks, raising one brow.

I try to cross my legs, but my dress is too short. Aidan's gaze darts to my hemline, and he bites his lip. Tucking my heels into the stool bar at the bottom, I sigh, unable to keep my wits when a man like Aidan Mixx is undressing me with his eyes. "I don't think so," I reply. "I'd have to go through my messages again."

Aidan chuckles and signals to the bartender with one finger in the air. He asks me what I'd like to drink and then orders for me. When my beverage arrives, I take a long sip immediately. Aidan clears his throat to get my attention. "You don't do this often despite what you want me to think. Am I right?"

"Maybe," I breathe out. "Yeah. You're right. I don't ever do this." The truth is a relief, and I turn my gaze to let him see my guard slip.

Aidan grins. It's a shrewd, predatory move that makes everything below my belly button tingle. My breath catches. His eyes slant in response to his smile, and I'm horrified to realize his facial symmetry is even more potent like this. When he's happy.

It's so bad or good it messes with my equilibrium, and I tilt off my stool and fall onto the floor—ungraceful, poisoned by testosterone.

Walking out of the garage, I'm greeted with a salty sea breeze and the squall of gulls in the distance. I knew this small beach town was the place for us when we moved away from Paul and Pamela. Paul didn't even fight me on the out-of-state move. He knew that Kendall wouldn't forgive him easily, and the embarrassment of his indiscretion was too much to bear anytime he tried to look at his own daughter. Paul would give her anything she wanted if it meant a second chance at being her father. He gave me the fastest divorce in history so we could move on quickly. Kendall wanted to move away with me, and she hasn't seen him since. He called on her birthday this past year, and she sat on the other end of the line while he wished her a happy birthday, tears pouring down her face. She thanked him through gritted teeth before she hung up the phone.

Turning my head toward the bay, I watch a ship bob on the horizon. Shielding my eyes, I pretend I'm on it, trying to picture the shoreline from that angle. It's a perfect, clear day, and aside from missing Aidan, I can't complain about much.

My cell phone chimes from the back pocket of my cut-off denim shorts. It's my friend, Jenny, asking if I'm free tonight. She wants to stop by later and share a bottle of wine and gossip. Everyone in a small town gossips. I'm thankful all of my drama happened away from this place, out of earshot of Bronze Bay residents. Jenny's daughter, Juliet, is one of Kendall's best friends, so the friendship blossomed with little effort, like any good friendship should. We can go weeks without speaking, but when we get together, it's like no time has passed at all. I text her back.

Come on over. LB is out of town this weekend.

Lover Boy is Aidan's nickname.

Her reply is quick.

I still can't believe you landed that man.

Her hesitance to accept I'm in a relationship with Aidan Mixx is out of concern. Everyone knows the SEALs that established a small Navy base down on the beach changed everything. They also know that several of the muscle-filled monsters tear through the town one woman at a time. They use the same tactics they use in battle—pop smoke before morning and you'll never hear from them again. Oh, and leave destruction in their wake. Lots of it.

I text Jenny.

We can talk about it over a bottle tonight.

A bottle or two. I'll ride my bike over. Juliet is spending the night at your house tonight.

Glad someone told me.

They don't tell us anything anymore, Magnolia. Don't feel bad. Be happy she still wants to be at home and not down at the beach getting blitzed on hunch punch.

I laugh out loud and slip my phone back into my pocket.

The kitchen window is cracked, and I hear Kendall

cry out in anger. Narrowing my eyes at the window, I try to see if I can glimpse her. I can't, so I move closer. Eavesdropping is a big part of parenting once your tween blooms into a hormone-filled teenager pushing adulthood. I push down the mom guilt and glide closer, trying to keep my old tennis shoes quiet on the pathway between the garage and my house.

"You're such a liar," Kendall shouts. "Like all men. Every one of you! All you do is lie!"

I swallow down the unease and peek in the window. Kendall isn't on the phone, she is shouting at someone in the doorway, someone just out of view. She's visibly upset, her face blotchy and red as she aims a finger toward the person. "You want me," Kendall accuses, jutting her chin up. I creep around to the back of the house. Laying my hand on the doorknob, I open the door and step into the mudroom and slide off my shoes. I pad barefoot into the kitchen, walking through the saloon-style doors that separate the entrance from the house.

My heart crawls into my throat and stops completely when I see the scene in front of me. Kendall has her arms wrapped around Aidan's neck, and they are…kissing. Heads tilted, his hands on her shoulders. "Aidan," I shout, tears stinging the corners of my eyes as the confusion turns into blazing fury. "What the hell is going on?"

Aidan pushes Kendall away, his eyes wide and focused on mine. "Magnolia. No. No."

I finally take a breath, unable to peel my eyes away from his face. Kendall runs out of the room, feet pounding on the stairs. "Aidan?" I repeat because I have no idea what to say.

My heart splinters, and it takes all of my control

not to collapse on the floor in a heap of broken bits. The same bits that the man in front of me helped put back together not that long ago. Thoughts of murdering the adult man I just saw kissing my seventeen-year-old daughter flood my brain in a flash. I push those thoughts down in an attempt to deal with the situation at hand. That is not him. This is not my Aidan Mixx.

He holds out two massive palms. "That was not what it looked like. It's not. Kendall is upset about something else." His low voice trips, and my heart sinks. Aidan's demeanor is wild, a side of him I've never seen. Obviously. "She's confused. I promise." Aidan shakes his head. "You can't think that I'd do that. You can't. Magnolia, please. Just listen to me explain for a goddamn second. Please. Ask her!" His tone is condescending. Like I'm the crazy one in this messed-up equation instead of him. The man with *his lips on my daughter*.

"Get out of my house," I say, the stone wall rising around my heart in a single second, returning to the cold, untrusting fortress it once was. "Now," I add, taking a deep breath.

"Please. I need to explain. Don't be ridiculous. You know me. I'd never hurt either of you," Aidan pleads, his throat working as he swallows. His beautiful eyes turn down in the corner, his lips still wet from my daughter's lips. Closing my eyes, I bring forth the person I have to be for Kendall.

"Get out of our life, Aidan. Get the fuck out and never come back here again. How could you?" Any explanation he could possibly give for his mouth on hers wouldn't suffice anyway. It wouldn't. No misunderstanding, no moment of bad judgment would explain it away.

I'm not sure how I make my legs work, but I forge forward and exit the kitchen, heading upstairs to find Kendall sobbing in her room. Aidan doesn't follow. I hear the chimes sound as he exits through the front door and his feet stomping down the front steps.

"Kendall," I say, shaking my head. "Tell me everything." Wrapping my arm around her, I pull her toward me. I close my eyes and shudder when I smell Aidan's cologne lingering on her skin. A scent I used to equate to happiness and satisfaction now makes my skin crawl.

"Mama," she replies, her eyes reflecting a pain I know all too well, yet don't understand at all. I'll never be able to fully dissect deceit. I never want to know what it truly means to live inside of lies. "I'm so sorry," she sobs.

"It's okay, baby," I soothe, kissing her head as she starts hissing out sentences I can't make sense of as her jagged crying increases in volume.

I tell her again that it will be okay, but I know she'll never be okay. I'll never be okay. This time it was my fault. I can't blame Paul for her collapse. This monster was inside our world because I brought him here. Because I let my guard down. I fell in love with the wrong man.

Again.

ONE
Aidan

The Past

She tumbles off the stool, and I can't help but glimpse the black lace panties staring back up at me. I didn't catch her quick enough, and instead of yanking her arm out of the socket, I lessened the blow by scooping in right before she hit the floor.

"I didn't peg you for a weak-in-the-knees type of woman. Maybe I'm underestimating my smolder?" I grin, sliding my hands up her slim waist as she stands. "I came and knocked you right off your feet." The panties are naughty lace, not the floral kind of lace you wear once you're comfortable with someone. My dick hardens, and the pit of need in my stomach enlarges.

Magnolia is horrified as she straightens herself, trying to yank on the dress that isn't nearly as short as she thinks it is. I've never seen a woman more uncomfortable than in this moment. I should tell her that it doesn't affect me, that it takes a lot to make my eyebrows rise, but I go the joke route instead to help counter her mortification. "No one saw," I add when she doesn't respond. "Trust me."

"I just fell," Magnolia gasps, waving her arm to the bar and the fact that everyone is, in fact, looking at us. "They'll be talking about this all week. I bet they all assume I came here drunk like old Verne down on the end," she hisses as she sits down again, shielding her eyes with one hand. Sighing, she rasps under her breath, "In this dress to boot. I never should have worn it."

Perfect opening. "Let's go back to my place and get it off you," I say, keeping the tone light. It would be easier if she agreed, if I could take her out of here and fuck her brains out. I guarantee she'd remember falling on my dick instead of off the stool. "You can't argue with that. You hate that dress." I wink when her gaze lights on mine.

Something in her eyes lights up. "No, I'm not that kind of woman," she deadpans.

My stomach sinks. Two hours of wasted time. An hour combined of total messages sent over the past three days and the hour I've spent at the bar. I use the app for one reason and one reason only. To fuck.

"You've got me all wrong." It's like the fall from the stool ignited her true personality. She opens her mouth to speak, then closes it again before finally speaking. "I thought I could pretend to be that kind of woman, but that's not me. This isn't me," she says, looking down at the dress, and then meets my gaze. "I'm sorry I wasted your time. I wanted to be this woman for you. You know? You're a beautiful man, but I think I proved how inexperienced I am with all of this. I fell off my chair because I don't know how to wear a fancy dress." She looks left when she says the dress part, and I call it a lie. She fell off her seat because she's uncomfortable around me. Her eyes are wild as she realizes the half-truth in her own words.

"Hey, it's fine. Really. I like that you don't do this a lot," I say.

"I do this never," Magnolia replies, emphasizing the last word.

I cock my head to one side. "Never?"

She shakes her head. "Not even once. My friend said this was a good idea. To meet a man who I knew very little about to kick-start the relationship...section of my life, but I'm in over my head. You're obviously very experienced in dating, and that makes it even worse. I need to work up to a man like you." She closes her mouth, and her eyes pop open. "That sounded awful. I'm not trying to be offensive."

I laugh. "I don't get offended, Magnolia. Tell you what? I'll help you get your groove back. Did an ex-boyfriend burn you?" If I know what I'm dealing with, I can feed her the game she'll play for. Everyone has something that's integral in another person. I'm an expert at pinpointing it.

She shakes her head, eyes closed. "I'm so embarrassed right now. Don't, please. I sound like a charity case or something."

"You're far too hot to be a charity case. I will enjoy every single second of being with you." Her eyes widen, and she turns her face toward mine. When her forehead wrinkles in confusion, I smile. "I'm serious. I will." No maybe about that.

"You're either that good, or you're being honest."

Or option C. I'm good at this because I do it all the time, and I'm far from honest.

Magnolia downs her drink and slides the glass away.

"Do you want another?" I ask, wiping sweat from my almost full beer bottle.

"I could have five and still be mortified. A reset button is what I need right now," she says.

Thinking for a second, I decide to put a little more effort into Magnolia Sager. She is more attractive than my usual date, and I have to admit her inexperience is charming. I'd be able to play with her in bed for hours. Days. I run my hand over my mouth as I narrow my eyes at her cleavage. Fuck yes. Worth every second. Sold.

There are always tables available here. Even on a Friday night. I tell the hostess I want the table for two in the back corner, away from the kitchen. I want to be alone with her, but this will have to do for now. The hostess bats her eyes and sticks out her ass as she tells me to follow her. I check out her ass and thank her once I'm seated. She leaves two menus, and I order a bottle of wine. White. Magnolia is a white wine drinker, I can tell.

It's exactly ten minutes later when Magnolia slips through the front door wearing a gauzy blue skirt and a black tank top, her hair is down, and her lips are free of lipstick. The wind blows her skirt a little when the door opens and closes, and my heartbeat pounds in my neck. I swallow down the unfamiliar sensation and begin to wonder where she's been hiding. Why haven't I seen her? How is she not taken? Married? In a small town like this, the beauties are the first to be swallowed in matrimony. I realized that straight away.

Magnolia smiles when she sees me watching her, takes a visible breath, and approaches our table, the hostess glaring daggers at her back. I stand as she nears. "Hi," I say when she's right in front of me. "I'm Aidan Mixx."

She nods. "I'm Magnolia Sager. It's nice to meet you." Her gaze flicks from my face down my body. "You are more attractive in person than in your photos."

I grin, and she swallows hard. "Funny you mention it, because you are the most beautiful creature I've ever seen. Are you actually human?" Her blush stains high on her cheeks. "Sit. I ordered a bottle of wine. I hope you don't mind."

"Red, I hope," she replies, sliding into the seat opposite mine.

I laugh. "White. I'll order a red, too." She's already throwing me off my game.

Magnolia smiles a megawatt, white smile. "My friend Jenny is wearing a hot pink bandage dress at the beach right now," she says, giggling. "This is the real me. I'm not the kind of woman I'm sure you're used to."

She's not. That's not necessarily a bad thing. I've had a few girlfriends sprinkled into my life. One I thought might turn into something, but my career deterred anything from becoming something more. I've hardened my heart against feelings. They complicate a life that is already full of complications. "What else do you know about me?" I ask, leaning toward her, my elbows on the small round table, my mind racing with images of her trading clothes with her friend on the beach.

She blows her hair out of her face and looks away. "I'm not a born and bred Bronze Bay local, so I'm not really in the gossip loop, but I have been here long enough to know about you. I do know you came here to open the Navy base down on the beach. I know you're in the special forces," she says, meeting my eyes. Her voice rises at the end.

"That a question?" I tilt my head to the side.

She shrugs. "Maybe?"

"I am."

"A Navy SEAL?" she asks, quieter this time, like she's whispering a secret. It's adorable.

I nod. "What else have you heard? It's sort of nice living in a small town. I barely have to talk. The town does it for me."

"I'm sorry. That's so rude of me."

Leaning my head to the side again, I grin. "I'm not offended. Remember? You can't offend me. I was being honest. You haven't gotten anything wrong yet. I'll correct you if you do. Go on," I reply, waving my hand.

"I'd rather you just told me," she says, casting her eyes down toward a glass of water.

The hostess, who is also the waitress, brings two long-stemmed glasses and opens the white wine. She pours for both of us and leaves, tossing a seductive look over her shoulder as she goes. If things with Magnolia turn south, I know who will be in my bed tonight.

There are only four other couples in the entire restaurant, and we're out of earshot of all of them. I rub my hands together. "I moved to Bronze Bay because the Navy told me to. I spent most of my life on the SEAL teams on the West Coast. San Diego," I say, watching her face as she processes my words. "I'm a military man. I don't settle down, and using an app to find dates is the easiest way for me to have company." I look to the right. The hostess is looking at me again. When I turn back to Magnolia, I know she hasn't noticed the other woman. She's oblivious. "When was the last time you went on a first date?" Hopefully by my intonation, she knows the word "date" implies more than just noodles and wine.

She drinks a sip of her wine, twirling the stem of the glass in her hand. Her long lashes fan across her cheeks as she watches the glass. She really is fucking beautiful. "Oh, give or take fifteen years," she says, laughing, a sarcastic noise. "Seriously, though." Her gaze meets mine. Truth.

Schooling my reaction is difficult. "Fuck," I say. "You're going to have to give me a bit more than that, Magnolia. Have you been hiding in a convent?"

She laughs. "This is the part where you run."

I down my wine, pour another one, and top off hers without replying, hoping she'll go on without further prompting.

"I'm divorced."

I nod. I'm thirty. About the age where it's normal to have a divorce under your belt. "And?" I ask, clearing my throat.

"How old is the average woman you date?" she asks.

Volleying my head back and forth, I calculate. "Twenty-five?"

"Is that a question?" Magnolia asks. "The hostess is nineteen. You like them young? Another thing I've been told about you SEALs that might not be a problem with other women, but it's a problem for me."

Her smirk is victorious, and I feel a wave begin to drown me. I'm in over my head. She hides things as well as I do. I swallow hard. Shit. "I guess the average varies," I say. "What does that have to do with us? You are clearly of age." He nods at my wineglass.

"I have a seventeen-year-old daughter. Almost an adult. Almost the same age as the waitress," she says, licking her lips. Her eyes narrow, waiting for my reaction. I've had years of practice hiding my emotions and feelings. Neutral. I need to find my best neutral persona. Magnolia continues, "I married my ex-husband directly out of high school. He left me for a nineteen-year-old. Expelling all of this information up front is probably a good way to never have a second date again, but I feel it's really important to be upfront if this is going to go further." She glances at the waitress once more and returns her gaze to mine.

I drink the second glass of wine and taste nothing, so I pour more. This is the part where I run. Far and hard and fast. "I'm into you. Just you. Where do you want this to go? Tell me how you envisioned this night going." Asking questions is a good way to gather your wits. I don't want to say something stupid, but I can't deny I'm intrigued.

She shrugs. "Jenny told me it was an app used primarily for one-night stands." Her blue eyes soften as her voice lowers. "I'm not sure I can do that, though."

Relief washes over me, and muscles I didn't even realize were tense ease back into my chair. This is a problem I can solve easily. Fuck, I might even be able to get her in my bed tonight, after all. I can deal with her baggage for one night. Better yet, I can forget her baggage for one night.

"You *can* do it," I say. "We are almost the same age, Magnolia. The fact you have a daughter is of little consequence to me. Honestly, my only reservation is how long it's been since you've gone to bed with a man. The concern being if I can be gentle enough."

Her lips are wet, and her breathing speeds up.

The waitress intrudes. "Are you ready to order?"

I'm about to tell her what I want when Magnolia interrupts. "You know what? Just bring us the check, please, darling." She meets my eyes. "That okay?"

I nod once. "Perfect," I growl.

TWO
Magnolia

A DEMON HAS POSSESSED my body. A wanton, sex-hungry she-devil with no morals and a fire between her legs. I'm embarrassed at my rash decision to leave the restaurant with Aidan, but I don't care enough to stop myself from getting into his car. It's a quick ride to his condo situated on the water. I texted Jenny and told her my plans, and all she texted back was the eggplant emoji and the peach. She obviously cares little about my well-being. My pink dress is probably inhibiting oxygen to her brain.

Aidan pulls his car into the small lot adjacent to his building and parks his car. A very nice, meticulously clean coupe that still has that new car leather scent. When you live at the beach, you realize how much of a rarity that scent is. My truck is filled with sand and somehow sticky with saltwater at the same time. His complex is a newer building with only a few units. Aidan puts the car in park and looks over at me vibrating in the passenger seat. "Just because you come inside doesn't mean you're going to leave ready to birth another child in nine months," he says.

"That's not funny, Aidan."

He holds up his hands. "Sorry. Was trying to lighten the mood. Casual sex is actually pretty fun. I can assure you that you'll leave feeling better than you have in years."

I glance his way again, and his profile takes me off guard. He is stunning. Truly. His boyish good looks are made more severe by the wolfish way he carries himself. Not only is he aware of that, he also owns it. It's why I have to take this opportunity. It may never happen again in my lifetime, surely not before a man like this still finds me attractive. My best years are behind me. This is the stuff of legends. Surely, no one would fault me, one night of poor decisions.

"I can't believe I'm doing this," I reply. "Let's go in before I change my mind and lose my nerve."

"Nerve has nothing to do with this," Aidan says, sliding his hand over the center console and onto my upper thigh, over my skirt. My breath catches, and I cough to hide it. He doesn't miss the cover; his grin tells me so. "Magnolia, the second I get my hands on you, you'll forget everything else. I promise."

"That's a bold promise," I whisper, warmth flooding between my legs.

"I don't make promises I can't keep. That's the first thing you should know about me."

"What else should I know about you?" I ask, rubbing my thighs together. There's no denying I'm not leaving this place without him extinguishing the desire. Call it a want. A need. Whatever you want. It's mine. I'll let myself feel guilt for my traitorous body tomorrow.

"Only that I'm about to rock your world."

I nod. That's all I really need to know for something like this, right? People have hooked up with each other knowing less. Much less. Then, why do I feel the need to ask him about his family and his career? Why do I want to pick his brain and find out if there's a good person lodged beneath the muscle and charm?

My mind is spinning in all directions as I step out of his car and follow him to his front door. He peers over his shoulder a few times, gauging my mood or guessing at what I'm going to say next. Probably taking bets on how fast I'm going to change my mind.

The summer sun hasn't set, and his condo is lit orange by the floor-to-ceiling windows that span the width of the room. There is a stairway right in front of us that leads up to the main living area. It's even brighter up here. "Doesn't it get hot in here?" I ask, glancing at all of the windows that would have curtains, blackout curtains, if I lived here. "You'd bake in here midday."

He rounds an island to the fridge. "I'm not here too much during the day," he explains. "Something to drink? I have everything."

"Wine," I say, a shiver running up my spine. "Red or white. Whatever you have open." What that really means is whatever the woman who was here before me liked best.

Aidan opens a new bottle of red, and while he pours, he says, "My bedroom is in the back, and I have curtains in there. The windows here in the living space have a tint." I'm listening to him speak while looking over the bay. It is a beautiful view. He extends the wine to me, his hand coming into my peripheral vision. "For you," he adds.

I thank him as I grab the glass, immediately taking a long sip. "It is quite nice at sunset, isn't it?"

"The best," he replies, opening his own beer. "There are so few of these units we had to fight for them. Some of the other housing options needed to be remodeled and worked on. That's not my thing at all." Aidan swallows down some beer and sinks down into a sleek loveseat that faces the windowed wall. His arm is perched along the back, open, an invitation.

Curiosity gets the better of me, and I sit down, my leg pressed against his. "What is your thing then? Outside of work and whatever that entails." Asking questions is easy when I'm not looking at his face, and when I have liquid courage sliding down my throat and a burning need flaming to life after what I thought would be eternal dormancy.

The arm behind me slips onto my shoulders, and when I turn my head up to glimpse his face, he's smirking. My stomach flips.

"Ironically my work is sort of my outside-of-work hobby as well. All the things I have to be good at for my job are the things I enjoy. I don't particularly like wasting time on things that won't serve me well."

Something about the last sentence doesn't sit well with me. "Like relationships?" I shouldn't care, shouldn't have asked, but the maturity motherhood has bestowed upon me will always win out.

"I've had relationships. A couple of them. My deployment and workup schedules typically don't allow for much else."

"But now you're able to…use the app," I reply, unable to explain more eloquently when he's looking at me with that dimple firing at my core.

Aidan grins, white teeth on display. "It does. I have

more free time now. Bronze Bay isn't exactly a hotbed for terrorists."

At the reminder of the war that raged in our country for years, a chill prickles my skin, and my mood diminishes. It was years of terror attacks, fighting war on American soil, sleepless nights, and heart-in-your-throat days when all you could do was watch the news and pray there weren't any bad guys hiding in your neighborhood—in plain sight. That's why there are so many new military bases scattered throughout the US. It's why the SEALs came to Bronze Bay, Florida.

I remember watching the news as they announced all the new cities around America that would house special operations forces. That was years ago, and a new way of life, of being on alert, is the new norm. "It must be a good change of pace then," I say, trying to keep my mind off the horror of the past and the memories that will be burned into my mind for the rest of time.

"It is," Aidan remarks. "What about you? Tell me about yourself."

Facing the water, I keep my gaze off him and on the horizon. "My house is right over there," I say, distracting myself and hopefully him. "See those lights?" I point to an outlet on the other side of the bay.

He nods.

"That's my neighbor's yard. You could probably get to my house quicker by boat than car," I joke.

"You're avoiding my question."

Sighing, I say, "I wasn't ready for actual conversation. I figured we'd get right to it," I explain, making a lewd gesture with my hands.

He pulls me in tighter. “Is that what you want then? To get right to it? I was trying to make polite conversation because that’s where it seemed you wanted to go.”

“No, no. I’m glad we’re talking. It was just unexpected, that’s all. I didn’t come up with any interesting facts to tell you about my life.”

“You didn’t have time to come up with lies?” he counters.

“I didn’t say that.”

He quirks one brow. “You didn’t have to.”

“That big, pastel purple Victorian house in town? The one that sells antiques?”

Aidan’s eyes light up. It’s hard to miss. Everyone knows it. It’s purple, and I didn’t have the heart to change it when I took it over.

“Yeah, that’s yours?”

“Magnolia’s Steals,” I reply dryly. “That’s my store. I collect and sell antiques. It was a casual hobby while I was married, but now it’s what I do full time. There’s an online store where a lot of my business takes place. I liked the idea of keeping an actual store where people could come in and touch things—see treasures from the past. I’m a sucker for a good story, and all of the furniture and jewelry and random bobs and bits have a story.” I shrug. It’s on the table. My life. Kendall and the shop. And my sordid breakup. “You basically know everything about me now.”

“Wow. That’s really impressive. I…like antiques.”

I snort. “Your house is the opposite of classic. It’s all modern, Aidan. You don’t have to pretend to like something just to get in my pants. Truth is, you were already headed there the second you smiled.”

"My smile?" Aidan teases, widening the very grin I'm talking about.

I look away. "That's the one."

"Here's the thing: this sofa might be considered modern now, but one day it will be an antique, right? It will tell the story of when I kissed the beautiful Magnolia Sager for the very first time."

"That is a pretty interesting story," I reply, cocking my head. "And how many other women were kissed for the first time on this modern loveseat?"

He coughs and drags his hand across his mouth to cover a smile. "You're the only one who matters."

"Right now," I deadpan. When his smile falls, I put him out of his misery. "It's fine. Honestly. I don't want anything long-term. Casual is something I've never tried before."

"You realize you are in the minority, then? Most women don't want to know or think about women who have come before them."

"And you? Do you want to think about the man who came before you?"

Aidan clears his throat. "Well, not really. I know enough to know that your ex didn't treat you properly. I may be into casual dating, but if I ever find a woman I want to keep forever, that's a game-changer. You can guarantee I'd be faithful. I'm honorable when it comes to promises and vows."

I nod. "That's one good quality," I say.

"One?" Aidan barks. "That's two in my column. You told me you liked my smile."

"That goes in the bad column. The smile will get me into trouble."

"The good kind of trouble, no?" he teases, biting his lip.

I stand with my empty wineglass and bring it to the kitchen. "That remains to be seen, Aidan Mixx," I say, grabbing the bottle and pouring another glass. "How am I getting home, by the way? Spending the night?" Spinning to face him, I waggle my eyebrows.

"No spending the night," he says, shaking his head, sliding his own glass onto the counter. "I'll drive you home."

"No sleepovers in casual dating? I thought as long as I was gone by morning, we'd be clear." That's what I've seen on sitcoms and movies. It can't be far off.

His smile is forced. "I don't sleep well with other people," he says, swallowing hard. And that may be the very first peek into his true personality I've seen tonight. A fact that, perhaps, others don't know about him.

When I go to take a sip of wine, he catches my hand before the glass touches my mouth. "Enough of that. I want you to be alert when we go back there," he says, hiking a thumb over his shoulder.

"Oh, are you my daddy? Telling me what I can and can't drink?"

Another lip bite. My head swims.

"I can be your daddy," he says. "I'd rather not, but I can be whatever you want me to be. Casual dating," he explains, raising both brows. "It's impressive. Whatever you want."

I set the almost-full glass down with a shaky hand. "Point taken," I say, nodding. "Show me your room?"

He grabs my hand and leads me out of the living area and down the short hall to his room. The space is darkened by curtains. Aidan hits a switch, and a dim glow illuminates the space. The bed is...antique. It's a double bed with a black, wrought iron frame. The finials on the corners of the bedposts are ornate, giving me all the clues I need as to age and make. As I take in my surroundings, I drag my hand over the beautiful frame. "This is nice. Where did you get it?" I ask, turning to meet his eyes.

"I acquired it when I became a SEAL. I needed a bed, and this one was sitting on the side of the road with a 'free' sign taped to it. Not the best story, but I've kind of grown attached to it, I guess."

Another truth. "Well, I think it's a great story, and I'm glad you kept it. It's in great condition," I say, examining the grooves and notches where it's been welded. The newer frames that try to replicate this style have cleaner lines. "It's a small bed," I say, offering a crooked smile. "Doesn't that inhibit your hobbies?"

"Now is the time that I show you how much I am not inhibited by the size of my bed," he counters, closing the space between us in two large steps. "Right?" he asks.

My breathing speeds up, and my stomach tightens. I'm in unknown territory, so even though I know this is a normal feeling, I can't control my hands as they clench and unclench by my side. Aidan runs his hands down my arms and ends with my fists inside his palms. He eases them open using his thumbs, laying his forehead against mine. "Just feel it," he says, leaning down to brush his lips against mine, shaking his head no.

"You lied," I say. "Weren't you supposed to kiss me for the first time out there?" I say, swallowing the lump in my throat. "On the sofa. In front of the windows?"

He backs me up, walking toward the bed. "I did lie. Only because I wanted to kiss you on my bed first."

"Why? Because I know how much it's worth?" I

say, grinning against his lips. We're not kissing, our mouths are merely lingering close, sharing breath, making me lightheaded with the need for more.

"No, because I kiss all of the women on the couch first. You'll be the first kiss in my bed."

"Well, isn't that romantic in a casual dating sort of way?" I counter, smiling in spite of the absurdity of it all.

"It's romantic in *every* sort of way," he says, laying me back on the bed. He drops a kiss on my collarbone and then my neck, his warm lips prickling my cool skin. Aidan holds himself off me as I scoot up on his bed until my head hits pillows. It smells like it's been freshly laundered, but at this point, I don't want to think of *why*. I need to push his conquests aside if I'm going to enjoy myself.

He pulls his lips away and rises to his knees. He yanks his shirt off and tosses me a lopsided grin. My mouth goes dry as I stare at him. "Are you even real? I didn't know muscles looked like that in real life," I manage.

He flexes his abs, and I count at least eight on first glance.

"It's part of my job," he replies.

"Right. You don't enjoy reaping the benefits of your job at all?" I ask, narrowing my eyes.

His grin spreads, and my heart skips a beat. "It does grant me some privileges I might not have otherwise. Like having *you* in my bed." Aidan unbuttons his jeans, keeping his gaze on mine. "So, you have less trouble later," he whispers.

A clear-headed Magnolia would tell him I'm a confident, capable woman who needs no help unbuttoning a man's jeans, but Aidan does possess another sense. A sex sense, and I would need help.

My skin feels like it's fire and ice as he moves a hand under my tank top. I'd watch if I wasn't so fascinated with how the lines in his biceps rise and lower under his skin anytime he moves even the slightest bit. My ex-husband isn't bad looking by any stretch of the imagination. He's long and lean and always stays in shape by running. Comparing Aidan and Paul would be like comparing apples and oranges—Chris Hemsworth to John Krasinski circa *The Office*, a non-comparison, really.

Aidan kisses my ear, gently nudging. "You're overthinking it," he says, sliding his hand up my stomach and under the front of my bra, his fingers splaying across my ribcage.

"How can you tell?" I say, my words a bit muffled by ragged breaths. "You're right, but how can you tell?"

Aidan brings his face in front of mine, his eyes dark, his tongue dragging across his bottom lip. "I'm good at this. I can tell." Another truth spoken with a rough, toe-curling edge.

I sigh, long and heavy. "I wish you weren't so good at this," I counter.

"Doubtful you'll hold on to that wish once we get started," he quips back, leaning down. "Close your eyes and part your lips."

I do as he orders, and he slides his hand over my breast and makes a pleased sigh the second his lips meet mine. He tastes of masculinity, the formidable, heady scent that invades your head right before a man invades your body. Reaching up to twine my fingers in his hair, I pull him closer so his bare chest is against me, and I'm fully consumed at all angles by him—his bulging arms by my sides, his pecs on my chest, and his mouth against mine, captivating all of my senses.

Aidan's tongue lashes out against mine, and this kiss turns deadly—sucking away any chance I had at keeping a level head. His dominating presence takes away any preconceived notions that I'll leave this room as the same woman who entered. My mind is a mottled mess, and my body is only attuned to his touch. He reminds me to keep my eyes closed, a murmur against my lips, in a brief pause, and he continues to kiss me and lavish me with his expert mouth and warm, purposeful touch.

The doorbell rings. Not in the cliché way in movies where a passionate coupling is broken up by a loud noise, it actually happens. Then again. And again when he doesn't respond right away. Aidan pushes a loud, annoyed breath through his lips and hops off the bed. I lean up on my arms, flushed and confused.

"Don't move a muscle. I'll be right back," he says, eyeing me down from the doorway.

Of course, as soon as he disappears from view, I follow him.

THREE
Aidan

STACEY? Tracey? Macy? Lacy? I can't remember her name, but her eyes are a familiar shade of fucking furious. She's in my doorway, peering around my body and up the stairs. "Hey, darling. I'm a little busy right now. What can I help you with?" I give her the smarmy drawl, but this bomb isn't defusing. Fuck.

"Who do you have in there tonight, Aidan?" the woman squeals out, hands clenched on her hips. "Huh? Who is hiding in there?" Her tone is loud and screeching as she directs her question upstairs. Fuck. Fuck. Fuck. Her blue, anger-hazed eyes meet mine. "You told me you'd call me. Did you change your number? I've been calling you."

"Baby, baby. You knew it wasn't more than a night," I say, trying to keep my voice down. "I don't do callbacks." It's kind of a lie. The fact that this woman isn't memorable in any sort of way tells me why I didn't call her back. I can't even picture what she looks like naked. The wildcat in front of me is making me nervous, so I can't turn around, but I sense

Magnolia is behind me, upstairs, listening to this madness.

"Don't do callbacks? What the fuck are you? A gigolo?" the wildcat yells.

Raising and lowering my hand, I signal for her to keep her voice down. "I have neighbors," I say. "Please keep your voice down." Shaking my head, I wrap my brain around this situation. If I were downrange, I'd have several plans ready to go. Backup plans for backup plans. Why should I treat this any differently? My mind spins a quick, effective plan.

"Bullshit. Your neighbors? You have a woman in there," she hisses. This is what fucking around in a small town has gotten me. I knew it would come to a head and my past women would collide. It was inevitable, but I didn't envision it happening on a night that seemed so different. "Don't you? Answer me! My friend told me not to go on a date with you, but I didn't listen because you seemed like a decent guy."

I cringe. Internally. I'll fix this in any way I can. Even if that means putting a Band-Aid on a gaping, oozing gash.

"Listen, sweetie, I don't have just any woman in there. *My* woman is in there. My girlfriend," I say, nearly choking on the last word. "That's why I didn't call you back," I explain, keeping my voice down in hopes Magnolia doesn't hear my seething lies. "I hope you understand, it's not personal. I didn't expect it. It happened suddenly." Wildcat is buying the story, I can see her heart breaking inside her eyes, the fury slipping —anger turning into despondent sadness. "She's important to me." Nail in the coffin.

Finally, she breaks eye contact, glancing down at the welcome mat she's standing on. "Oh," she says.

"You could have called me back even if it was to tell me this. Now I feel stupid."

Thank you. Thank you. Thank you. I sigh, making sure not to make any noise, and close my eyes in relief.

"I hope she can fix you," Wildcat sneers.

No woman can fix me. Not in a million years. Not after all of the damage that's been done. I'd never tell anyone that. Especially not this insignificant woman trying to make me feel bad about my life. Instead, I nod and screw up my face in what I hope looks like sentimental agreement. "Sorry for the confusion," I say. "Have a good night…"

"Polly. My name is Polly," she says, shaking her head, then turning on her heel, tail tucked, all the way back to whatever section of hell she rode in from.

"Fuuuuuuuck," I hiss out under my breath and steel my nerves to try to amend my night with Magnolia. Closing the door slowly, I try to formulate something intelligent to say, a way to explain away the things I said and my whoring ways. Magnolia knows I'm not a one-woman man, maybe she'll just shrug and attack me with her sweet pussy. I walk up the stairs, one at a time, when I usually bound up them in a couple leaps.

When I get to the top, I'm met with her piercing, accusing gaze. It's anything but indifferent. She's scrutinizing me. "Am I going to fix you or let you stay broken?" she says, pressing her lips into a firm line, feeding me Wildcat's words. Her tank top is askew, and her hair is a brown, sexy mess. My mouth waters and my cock throbs. I grab it to reposition it, and her attention slides down. Yes, familiar territory.

"Fix me," I say, trying to set the mood where I'd like it. "If you can." I quirk one brow.

"I'm your girlfriend, huh?" she replies, tilting her head to the side.

I blink slowly and run a hand through my hair. She watches my abs as I move. "You weren't supposed to move a muscle. Or hear any of that, for that matter. She was upset."

Magnolia crosses her arms across her chest. "She was screaming. How could I not hear that? The question remains, am I really your girlfriend after one date, after one kiss? Or do I tell my friends you lie when confronted? When you feel uncomfortable?"

Sweat beads on my forehead even though my air conditioner is set to freeze my balls off. My breathing quickens. She better be the best lay of my fucking life. "Are you blackmailing me into being your boyfriend?" Not without my permission, but it wouldn't be the worst thing in the world to be attached to a woman in Bronze Bay. Perhaps it would even clear my bad name if I gave it a real shot. I tick through the women I've been with, and there's only one who could hold that torch. She's standing in front of me right now. Why Magnolia? I know she'd never show up at my front door with a pitchfork. She has a family. People she cares about and has to maintain manners for.

"Would I really blackmail the man who I want to give me orgasms? That would be bad for business."

I smirk, blowing out a breath. "Business?" I ask, approaching her. "That's what this is?"

"I need instruction on dating and sex in this decade, and you need…someone who has a good reputation," Magnolia returns, backing away, her bare feet soft on the tile floor. My cock does that thing when it lets me know I'm not in control anymore, standing up so proudly that readjusting would be a waste of time.

"Well, well, you are far shrewder than I thought you were capable of," I counter.

"Just because I haven't been with a man since my ex doesn't mean I suck at business transactions. I'm not a kid," she says, reminding me of the average age of the women I've been with up until now.

"How do I know you have a bad reputation?" I ask, lowering my lashes when I'm standing in front of her and can scent her in my oxygen.

Magnolia leans up on her toes and juts her chin up. I kiss her on the mouth, a wet, slow, lavish gesture. "Face it, all you really need is one woman who sticks around. A woman you're seen with. A woman who isn't different every night of the week. A woman who has good standing in the community and who will be faithful."

I realize what this means, and it's still a little shocking. I have to be faithful. One woman. Just one.

"I give you lessons on dating, and you give me consistency."

She tilts her head back and forth. "Something like that."

"You're that desperate? Don't get me wrong, I'm probably the best teacher you can find in this town, but you're also taking on *my* bad reputation."

Magnolia narrows her eyes. "Not if I fix you."

I narrow my eyes in return. "Ah, I see." All at once I'm not sure Magnolia Sager can't fix me. The bad, dark feelings cloud my mind, and I know I have to do something to remedy that. Do what I always do.

Clearing my throat, I pull her close and slide her tank over her head and toss it on the ground. I do the same with her bra. The sunset is glowing on the horizon, filling my glass box with orange light, highlighting her beautiful body. I press a kiss on the center of her chest and then another on her lips. She's hesitant to release me, and that knowledge gives me power. Pulling away, I pin her with a crooked grin as I hit my knees.

Those black lace panties come down with her skirt, and she inhales sharply when her body is fully exposed. I gasp sharply when I see her bare, for me, standing in front of me with more confidence than I expected. I'm not sure what I thought she'd look like naked. I'm usually a pretty good judge by looking at a fully clothed body. Her hips are narrow, and her stomach is flat. Her breasts are shapely and symmetrical, still full and more than plentiful. Her legs have the curves of a runner. I can't see her ass because her pussy is in my face, but my hands slide around, and the firmness feels like a fucking textbook round ass.

I swallow hard. "You are fucking perfect, Mags," I say. In this dazed moment, I briefly forgot she doesn't like to be called anything but Magnolia. I can't form sentences, or I'd correct myself. Running my hands over her body while she breathes heavily is all I can manage at the moment. She hasn't been touched like this in who knows how long. If I can manage, I need to take this slowly, letting her savor every sensation. Swallowing hard, I mentally ready myself for the challenge. Not that I'm usually a taker in the bedroom, but at the moment I'm feeling a bit over my head with regard to my self-control.

Glancing up to her face, I see her eyes are closed, her lips slightly parted. She opens her mouth to say something, then closes it again. Standing, I grab her hip bones and back her up to the living room until she's against the sofa and no longer a fall risk. Magnolia looks up at me, and the trust I see there churns my stomach—forces the truth in the intimacy at play. As a whole, if you ignore the intimate details of fucking, it can be just fucking. If you let emotion slip in, even just a little bit, it turns everything into something else entirely. That's what I avoid. That's why I don't remember what Wildcat looks like naked. Why I don't recall who I slept with last weekend. Why my heart is beating out of my chest right now at the realization that I'm letting it slip…for a woman I barely know because she deserves intimacy. Connection. Even if I'm the fucked-up sap who has to give it to her.

With her neck in both of my hands, I lean her head back to give myself a better angle to kiss her senseless, my thumbs controlling her chin. Her skin is smooth, her cheeks pink, and the scent of her arousal urges me on, regardless of my hesitance in giving in, breaking my own rules. The kiss is deep, and I'm controlling every nuance, and I think maybe if I can dominate her completely, I won't end the night a fucked-up mess. Gliding my lips over to her ear, down her neck, I end with one nipple in my mouth and drag my lips over to capture the other one. Magnolia moans, her hands fisting the back of the couch.

Swallowing hard, I grit my teeth against the urge to flip her around, slide my dick home, and fuck her wild. Magnolia sighs, relishing the moment, and with tight control, I dip my head lower and kneel, pressing kisses on her flat stomach as I part her legs with one hand. Her thighs tighten as she spreads her legs opening me to her soft, wet playground. At first, I play with her gently, testing, rubbing, and gliding to find out what makes Magnolia tick. When I let my middle finger slip inside the warm tightness, she screams out, clutching my hair in her hands. "You like it when I'm inside you," I say, licking my lips as her pussy clenches around my finger.

"Yes. Inside me," she repeats back to me, voice harsh. Magnolia scoots back so she's sitting on the back of the sofa and opens her legs farther, an invitation. Her gaze dips down just as I look up at her, and her face is this masterful mix of pure pleasure and blatant honesty. "Basically any which way you can touch me, I like," she adds when she realizes she has my undivided attention.

"Noted," I say, leaning in to kiss her clit, my gaze on hers, my finger working inside her. I want to see the second my lips close around her. Magnolia buckles under the pleasure, and I scoot in to place her legs over my shoulder so I can eat her more easily. Taking out my finger, I insert my tongue into her as far as I can and begin lapping at her with a furious pace. Her thighs clench my neck, and I'm surrounded by the scent of her impending orgasm. It's slick folds and sexy moans, and my dick is straining against my jeans in the most unbearable way.

"I'm coming," she announces moments later, her words a sigh of relief. She runs her hands through my hair and leans her head back when the orgasm rocks her body. I feel the waves on my tongue strong and deep, and I'd give anything to feel that clenching on my shaft.

"You look good coming," I announce when her legs have turned to jelly and her grip has loosened. Sucking at her clit now that it's sensitive, I swirl my tongue on the nub. She moves her hips against me, obviously not done with my attentions. "How many more do you think I can give you?" I say, breaking my mouth from her pussy. When she whimpers, I slide a finger back in and watch her eyes roll back in her head as I rub her G-spot.

Magnolia heaves a long, beautiful sigh. "I'm afraid to answer that," she responds, taking her legs off my shoulders to stand on her own, effectively cutting off access to my buffet. "It could go on and on. It's been so long since I've felt..." she stutters. "Anything remotely close to that." Her face goes solemn.

I take her in my arms, picking her up. "What's the mean face for?" I ask, walking her into my bedroom.

"Mean?" she asks, pulling away to look at my face.

She looks away quickly. "'Mean' might not be the right word. I rocked your world, and you're looking a little glum, that's all."

She sighs and buries her face in my neck. "I didn't realize what I've been missing, that's all. All of this time alone. Hell, all of the years I was married, it was never about me. Not like that. Like what you just did," she says. "I feel so stupid."

When we're in my bedroom, I drop her onto my bed. She grabs the headboard, pretending to be overly interested in it. Fuck. Fuck. Fuck. Fuck. All of this is making me crazy. This night is already shot to fucking hell, anyway. "He was a moron, you have nothing to feel stupid about." Right? I don't know the guy, but he must be some special sort of stupid to cheat on a woman like her.

Magnolia sighs long and exasperated. "It should have been a sign," she says under her breath.

"Get used to it, honey. Tonight, it's only about you."

When her gaze finally meets mine, she brightens at my words. My attention. Her face like the goddamn sun after years of darkness. I've never wanted to claim a naked body more than I want hers right now.

Not because I've marked her as unfuckable for the night, either.

Because I've never cared enough to realize there is worth in waiting.

I dive into the bed and bury my face into her wet pussy. I settle in for the night even if my dick is anything *but* settled. When she comes for the third time on my nose and face, she screams my name so loud that I come in my motherfucking pants.

There's the difference. There's the fucking difference. Groaning, I drag my slippery lips up her body. Her eyes are closed when my mouth lands on hers.

I kiss her with my eyes open.

FOUR

Magnolia

My marriage didn't disintegrate over time. It imploded in one horrifying, self-actualizing moment. I had no idea Paul was unhappy—no blatant signals he was cheating on me. Sure, over time we settled into the comfortable familiarity of a worn-in relationship, but my mistake was thinking that was normal. Didn't all couples say "hello" and "goodbye" and "what's for dinner?" Isn't the lack of passion and fire between two bodies bound to dwindle after years of the monotonous grind of running a family business and parenting a child? The simple answer? No. It shouldn't. Ebbs and flows in a marriage are completely normal. Ebbing for years without ever feeling the rush of a flow is a proverbial death wish. *I should have known.*

The last year and a half of our marriage, he came home late almost every night when I knew the workload like the back of my hand and couldn't find a reason for his tardiness. There wasn't that much work to do after five p.m. Not by a long shot. But he kissed me square on the mouth, smiled, and asked me what was for dinner moments after coming through the door. Normal. I didn't see the symptoms of chinks in our armor. I didn't know I was supposed to be looking for them. Paul's affair is not my fault, I know that. That mistake lies squarely on his shoulders. Accepting a halfhearted offering of his love *is my fault.*

I was naked, in the shower when he busted into the bathroom to tell me Kendall caught him having sex with Pamela. He apologized so many times, his words eventually faded. I still had conditioner in my hair and only one leg was shaved. Par for the course, though. A divorce feels like unfinished business even when it's final. I shave that leg first now as if I can prevent my world from being rocked by keeping it smooth.

Sleeping isn't an option. I will be up for the rest of the night. I can't get Aidan's face out of my mind. Or his body. Or the fact that my inner thighs are stinging from the stubble burn of his scruffy face hours later. My core clenches at the reminder of all of the orgasms he gave me with his mouth and fingers. He wouldn't let me reciprocate the act, and something about that makes me feel guilty. It also makes me feel all kinds of butterflies in my stomach. I lie awake in my king-sized bed, staring at the ceiling, piecing together the reasons my marriage would have never worked even if Paul hadn't cheated. We had a child who connected us, but that doesn't mean we had a connection. The real kind, one that sizzles and pops and causes an ache deep in your chest.

Recognizing that Aidan is a horrible man to fall for was made even clearer when Polly showed up at his door demanding...him. Other women desire him. It's a risk to give anything except my body to Aidan Mixx, and yet I feel it happening, felt it happening all night long. Every touch held an unspoken promise of pleasure I know I'll never tire of. More than his body and his touch were his words. He told me I was desirable. That I was worthy of his attentions. By claiming me as his girlfriend, even if the scenario is pretend, he's affirming I'm good enough to be his, and everyone around him can witness it. Warmth spreads through my body when I think of the words he said when he dropped me off at my front door. *I've never wanted to call someone mine more.*

Clutching the sheets, I roll to look out the window that overlooks the bay. I have a clear shot of his bright white condo complex lit with several megawatt lights that highlight the shoreline and docks. "You're right there," I say, realizing how this town got a touch smaller with the knowledge that I can look out my window and know he's there. I wonder if he's looking over here. I wonder if he's awake. If he's regretting our deal, or if he's thinking about me. It's hard to think he might be. I'm another woman in his laundry list of conquests, and he just joined an exclusive club formerly known as Paul's.

I'll get used to it. I can do this.

I blink a few times as my eyes get heavier. My cell phone's dull glow signals a message. I grab it from my nightstand and unplug it from the charging cord. Aidan put his number in my phone before we left his house. His name flashes as his initials, AM.

His text reads,

I can't sleep.

I reply.

I can't sleep. Probably for different reasons though.

If not being able to get a chick out of your head is the reason you can't sleep, then we're on the same page.

I blush and swallow hard, rolling to my back, the phone hovering over my face.

You can't stop thinking about me?

Aidan texts back.

I never said it was you.

Oh, it's Polly then? She was a bit feistier than I was.

I fire back, grinning from ear to ear.

You're full of jokes.

So are you.

Your body is all I can see when I close my eyes. Then my dick gets hard. Sleeping is impossible with a hard-on. In case you were unaware of that fact.

This is why sleepovers are nice. If you were next to me right now, you could just roll over, and game on.

My core clenches again, and I flush, a reaction to

merely thinking about Aidan naked and his attentions focused on me. I add,

If it wasn't obvious, I'm not good at dirty talk.

I need the opposite of dirty talk to calm myself down. What are you doing later?

Swallowing hard, I try to think where this is going. There is no way in hell Kendall can know I'm seeing someone regularly. She can know I'm dating casually, but to what extent needs to be a well-guarded secret. Kendall feeling secure, loved, and happy is what I will always focus on first and foremost.

Kendall has a parade. It starts at Bronze Bay High School and goes through Main Street at lunchtime. I'm helping decorate the float in the morning. I'll be dead to the world without sleep, but that's what coffee is for, right?

Any plans for the evening?

I could be persuaded to accept plans for the evening.

Kendall asked permission to sleep over at Jenny's with Juliet, so I have the night free.

Aidan texts,

A tour of Magnolia's Steals? Then a walk on the beach? Cocktails in hand.

Smiling, I reply,

Are you hunting for any specific antique treasure?

I am.

Give me some details so I can look into my inventory beforehand.

Sculpted tail. I'm okay if it's a little leaky. A smooth finish. Something that responds to only my touch, though.

Pressing my lips together, I try to stifle my laughter, but it resonates in my bedroom louder than it should.

I think I might have something that fits that description. If not, I'm going to auction next week. I'll keep my eyes peeled.

Auction?

You know, where people sell their old things? Typically, it is stuff left over from estate sales, or someone dies and has a house filled with treasures that their family is trying to sell off. I love a good auction.

Oh, okay. I had something far more nefarious in mind when you said auction.

No one is selling sex at the auctions I attend,

I reply, rolling over again.

Aidan's message bubbles up.

You just gave me a hard-on again.

You don't have to pay me for sex. I'm your girlfriend, right? Isn't that part of the gig? I give it to you for free?

The gray bubble pops up and disappears for a few moments. He's struggling with how to respond. He begins typing again, and his message arrives.

How long is our relationship arrangement scheduled for?

My stomach sinks.

How long do you think it should be? How long do you need to hold a relationship to fake everyone out and make them think you're a changed man?

He is the prime example of what happens when you screw your way through a small town. You're left to focus on damage control.

We can play it by ear?

Your hard-on disappeared that quickly, huh?

I try joking.

No, it's still here. Sort of shocking, actually.

Sleep never comes while I talk to Aidan until sunlight begins to invade my room. The words always drifted back to sex and his dick, but in between were real flashes of two people getting to know each other. He's estranged from both of his parents, and he has no siblings. He didn't want to admit to that, but he did after I volleyed information he wanted. There's more to that, to his childhood and the reasons he isn't on speaking terms with his parents, but he closed that topic quickly, and I was left with a heap of questions and a bad taste in my mouth.

Is that how Kendall will view her childhood? Will she never speak with her father again? Will he become an estranged memory that is painful to talk about? A man she doesn't claim. A man who will never be in her life to celebrate in her victories and cheer her through failures? A chapter in a dark place in her life she won't share with the man she falls in love with without prodding? My stomach flips, and I hate that I recognize the hurt in Aidan and compare it to what Paul did to Kendall.

My daughter bounds into the room after knocking furiously several times, a rule we both formed when we moved into the new house. I give her space, she gives me mine, and we knock before we enter each other's respective spaces. "Momma!" Kendall cries out, a bouquet of youthful energy. "Are you awake?"

"Good morning, baby. I'm up," I croak, rolling to look at her. She's wearing a Mickey Mouse T-shirt with googly eyes, a souvenir we picked up when we went on vacation to Orlando, Florida, when she was five. She begged for the shirt while at Disney World. I bought it several sizes too big for her at the time, and still to this day that shirt is worn as soon as it's clean. She says because it's old and soft, but I know the real reason she loves it. It's my line of business. She loves the memory attached to it. A feeling of love and fullness, a grasping for a time when things were simpler, and her family was full and untainted by infidelity.

"We need to swing by the hardware store before we head to school. I told Juliet I'd pick up gold spray paint. Ms. Jenny and Juliet left here early to get started on the float."

Kendall sits on the edge of my bed, gazing out the window. "How many cans do you think you'll need?" I ask, sitting up, hoping I don't look like the changed woman I feel inside. I assumed everyone was asleep when I crept in last night. Jenny spent the night here with the girls. Our house is big, old, and drafty. It has more guest rooms than we'll need, but because of the age, location, and the price was right, it's ours forever.

Kendall sighs. "I don't know. Four? Maybe five? It's for the skirt of the float. I ironed my skirt so you don't have to," Kendall says. "I couldn't sleep, so I already ate, too."

I didn't hear her. Not one sound to indicate she wasn't peacefully asleep in her bed tucked in tight. "Oh," I reply, swallowing hard. Laying a hand on her shoulder, I say, "Everything okay? You want to talk about it?"

Her eyes narrow as she looks at me. "He called me last night," Kendall says, eyes watering. "While you were out. I don't want to talk to him, Mom. I don't want to ever talk to him again."

"That's your decision. It's your right, Kendall. Don't talk to him until you're ready. Remember what the therapist said? It's all up to you, honey."

A tear drops. "I talked to him last night." She says the words like it's her last confession. My heart squeezes.

"What did he say?" It's a morbid curiosity I'll never outgrow, I think. You think you know every single thing about a person only to come upon a day when the man you once loved is a stranger. I'll always be interested in his life regardless of how much he hurt me. It's irrational, I know, but the hope is one day it will merely be curiosity without any emotions attached to the update.

"He's marrying Pamela," Kendall says, scoffing when she says her name. "He asked me to come to the wedding. Told me it would be a fresh start. The start that should have been. He wants me to pretend I didn't walk in and see him cheating on you. With that awful woman...girl, whatever she is."

I can't help it. My stomach heaves at the knowledge. I knew they were still together, but I assumed he'd grow tired of Pamela in the way he grew tired of me. Never for a second did I think he would move on with her in a marriage capacity. Live together? Sure. Give her the same vows he gave me? "Excuse me, honey. I'm not feeling so well. One second."

Shuffling across the hardwood, I enter my bathroom and close the squeaky door and vomit into the toilet. It's unfortunate I can't control it, I can't hide my shock and horror at this knowledge for Kendall's sake, but it's too much to hide. Too much.

She knocks on the door. "Mom, it's okay. I told him I'd rather die than go to his wedding to that whore," Kendall says through the closed door.

I squeeze my eyes shut and swallow down the acrid taste of vomit. "Don't talk like that, Kendall. That's a horrible thing to say." Thank God she said it. Thank God. "You need to call and apologize to your father." Thank God I have her. Thank God she hates him.

Pamela is a fucking whore. Her father is a horrible human. The worst. "Do you understand me, Kendall?"

She stays silent, waiting to talk to me to my face, I'm sure. I splash water on my neck and cheeks and brush my teeth quickly, staring at the person in the mirror. He is marrying Pamela. How can he do this? Asking Kendall to be a part of that atrocious abomination of a day? I'm going to call him as soon as I have the house to myself. Give him a real piece of my mind.

I open the door, and Kendall flies into my arms.

"I don't want to apologize to him. He's not a nice person. You told me to always be kind. If I can't be kind, then be silent. I don't want to be silent. I want him to know that he hurt me. That he hurt you. He doesn't deserve to be happy."

He doesn't. Anger and rage boil to the surface. I hug Kendall, tucking my head into her hair, inhaling the scent of her fruity shampoo. "I'll talk to him. You don't have to go, okay?"

She nods. "You should have come to me when you couldn't sleep, Ken," I say, pulling her long hair into a ponytail, peering into her eyes. "I'm so sorry you have to deal with this."

"Everyone has shit in their life," she says, shrugging. "My shit just happens to be one-half of the pair that gave me life."

"Don't curse," I say. "It's not ladylike."

Kendall smirks. "He is shit, though."

Shaking my head, I pull her back in for another hug. "He is," I admit. "But good or bad, he is your father, and you'll have to deal with him at some point. I'm not saying now, because that's bad form on his part, but eventually, Kendall, you will have to look at him, and despite everything he's said and done to you, you'll have to forgive him. Not for him. For you. For you, honey." I sigh. If only I could take that advice. Only minutes ago, I was basking in the glow of the possibility with Aidan, and once again Paul has dragged me back down to planet Earth. Reality.

"Maybe on my deathbed. Or his," Kendall replies, pulling out of my grasp. She sits on my bed hard, bouncing, her hands tucked under her thighs. The eyes on the Mickey Mouse shirt move up and down as she bobs, and the pit returns to my stomach.

Swallowing hard, I tell her, "Go get dressed. We can stop by the coffee shop for tea and pastries before we go to the hardware store. That sound okay?"

Kendall wipes under her eyes. "Thanks, Mom. I'm sorry I had to tell you that. I didn't want him to spring it on you. Better from me than him."

"When did you get so old and wise?" I ask, smiling sadly. Approaching her, I tuck her hair behind her ears like I did a million times when she was a wild toddler. "I'm okay, honey. I promise. My stomach wasn't feeling good all night. I think it's why I slept so poorly."

"My therapist says it's part of the process. Putting my feelings aside to think about what others might be feeling. And since there's no way I'm putting myself into his smelly shoes, I'd rather put myself into yours. I'm sorry, Mom. I was so wrapped up in what I saw." She looks off and enters the dark place I hate with a violent passion. "And how that made me feel, that I didn't stop to think how awful it would feel to actually be married to a man who did that."

There are moments when your children speak, and you realize a level of maturity developed that wasn't there only days, perhaps moments, before. This is one of those moments, and I'm not prepared for it. Not prepared for it because Kendall is moving through the grief process more eloquently than I am. Sure, it was my marriage, but for all intents and purposes, she lost the father she thought she had. "I love you, baby. Thank you for that," I say, kissing the top of her head. "I'm doing great. Don't worry about me, okay? I'm so over it. The past is the past."

She hops off my bed and skips out of my room, lighter than when she entered. My heart is a little darker for it, but that's okay. I'll take it if it means she doesn't have to carry it. I allow myself to cry in the shower, the hot water splashing around me to hide the emotions I'm trying to bottle up. Pamela didn't just take my husband, she stole the happiness I thought I had. I take my time cleaning my body. With every glide of the razor on my legs, I find new resolve. A steely mission to not let their marriage affect my life.

I paste the smile on my face, the one that tells everyone I'm okay, when I meet Kendall in the kitchen. Then again when I order our drinks at the café, and still when I'm at the hardware store. I pretend to be okay while I laugh and paint the float with my daughter. I tell her how beautiful she looks as I zip up her cheerleading uniform in the locker room and watch her board the parade float. I smile and wave to her and her friends, my grin wide and encouraging.

When Kendall sets off, the float disappearing into the distance to the sound of the marching band, the charade ends. I know Kendall is safe with her friends and heading to Jenny's directly following the conclusion of the parade. I retreat to Magnolia's Steals, and surrounded by thousands of stories from the past, both happy and sad, I fall apart completely.

FIVE

Aidan

MAGNOLIA DIDN'T RESPOND to my texts asking if we were still on for tonight, but that didn't stop me from driving to her store. When I arrive at Magnolia's Steals, I hear the stereo blasting before I enter the lilac-hued two-story house. The "closed" sign is in the window, but the door is unlocked. I enter as quietly as possible, closing and locking the door behind me. The scent of wood polish and lavender hit me at once. It's a scent that I'll associate with Magnolia from this moment forward. It's not strong, it's a perfect blend.

As I take in my surroundings, my heart begins pounding out a staccato. Following the loud music brings me to a back room, hidden by a narrow staircase. The door is closed. My hand on the knob, turning it, I gently push the door open. She's sitting with her back to me, her head on the desk in front of her, a small jewelry box of some sort in front of her.

I call her name once, and she turns to my voice, her face red and swollen. "Aidan. What are you doing here?" She looks down at her watch and then at the clock on the opposite side of the room.

"What's the matter?" I ask, trepidation laced in my question. Dealing with emotions is not my specialty, nor something I'd choose to deal with if given the options between tear gas, bullets, and emotion. "Are you okay?" It's a stupid question given her appearance, but one I have to entertain because as the only other human in the room, it's my job.

She reaches over and turns off the radio. "What does it look like?" She spins on the stool to face me. "I'll never be okay," she says. Rubbing her eyes, she shakes her head. "I can't believe you're here. I'd forgotten completely. I was here by happenstance. I couldn't be at home in case Kendall went back there. I'm a mess today, so I'm hiding."

Tentatively, I approach, my heart in my fucking throat. I extend the bottle of wine. "Will this help the mess at all?"

She scoffs. "It's a good start. Grab that gadget over there. It's an old corkscrew." I let my gaze pan over the table filled with shit I have no clue about and find the only curly thing she could mean. I hand it to her. "You can leave now. You don't want to be with me tonight. It's going to be sloppy and crude. Thanks for this," Magnolia says, shaking the bottle of wine, her hand wrapped around the neck. "You saved me a trip down to the general store, where I would have made a fool of myself. Again. The town gossips would have loved that."

Sighing, I take a step back. "How sloppy? I'm into sloppy," I admit. "But if we're talking about crying while fucking, I may have to bow out gracefully. Hard pass."

She laughs loudly and then pops the cork. "Maybe you need to stay for a bit. You make me laugh."

That's a nice ego boost even if it seems like she's putting me in the friend zone. "I'll stay as long as you want me to stay. You are my plans for tonight, Magnolia."

She rubs her lips together and shakes her head. "I look like shit. Just my luck."

Raising one brow, I comment, "You've looked better, but it's obvious you're upset. Do you want to tell me who to kill now or later?"

"You'd kill for me? Awwwww, you're such a good fake boyfriend," she replies, standing to open a free-standing cabinet in the corner. She takes out two wine-glasses that remind me of a stained-glass window. She blows on them and rubs the rim against her shorts, one on each side. "These are expensive. Let's not break them, okay? Also, I might take you up on that whole killing idea. I need a little more time to ponder it." She pours the wine sloppily, trying to fill them quickly.

"That serious, huh?" I ask, accepting the glass of wine she thrusts into my hand. "This place is amazing, by the way. I've never been inside. I've only seen the extravagant window displays. You do a really good job." Every season is a display more extravagant than the next. They remind me of the intricate displays you see in NYC during Christmas—the attention to detail is absurd, and people come from all over the state to crowd around and catch a glimpse of whatever the creation of the season happens to be. When she first told me this place was hers, I felt stupid I didn't make the connection, and then I was impressed because of the displays.

She smirks, sipping from her glass. "The Christmas

one last year," she says, glancing to the side. "It will be hard to beat."

"Yeah, the Christmas tree made from old wrought iron cooking utensils," I say, hoping the change in subject will sway her mood. "What do you have in mind for the next holiday?"

She sits back down on the stool, shaking her head. "I have no earthly idea."

"I'm sure you'll think of something," I manage, eyeing her hesitantly as she drains the entire glass, her eyes glassed over.

She shakes her head. "Are you staying then?"

"I said as long as you want me to." There's a chair stacked in the corner. I grab a leg and turn it right side up and set it next to her.

She swallows hard. "No matter what I say? You'll stay?"

My stomach churns even as I nod. "Magnolia. You can't scare me." I hold up a hand. "Maybe you could if you were sloppy drunk, fucking me while holding a weapon. I'd be a little uncomfortable then. I can't be sure, though, because thinking about it is getting me a little excited." I shrug.

She slides me a half smirk. "You won't even be able to give me advice because you're just a...whore," she says. "I don't mean that in an offensive way, but in a factual way, you know?"

"Ouch," I reply. "Bitter about a man, then?"

"It's not you. It's men in general. And their whore women who ruin lives."

I swallow hard. Uncharted territory means I have no idea what the fuck to say, and she's right. I won't have advice. This is shit I don't have to deal with when my only companions have been twenty-something one-night stands, though I do have enough shitty life experience to keep conversation broad. "Your ex?"

"He's marrying Pamela. The woman he cheated on me with. The woman Kendall saw him physically fucking on *my* dining room table. Marrying her. Giving her *my* vows." She takes the bottle from the desk and fills her glass and then mine. Shaking her head, she closes her eyes. "I didn't think it would bother me this much. It was a possibility, of course, but I thought she was just his first stop on the adultery train."

"Vows don't mean anything, Magnolia. Not from a man who breaks promises. I'm sorry you're hurting, but you should know that the vows he will give Pamela are just as weak as the ones he gave you. That's not anything special. It's lies disguised as vows." I sip my wine, looking anywhere except her eyes. They're boring into me, trying to eat my soul. "If it makes you feel better, you should know she's just a stop on the adultery train. There will be other women—a second, a third, and probably a fourth and a fifth. Consider yourself lucky you're out now and don't have to wonder. Poor Pamela will do nothing but wonder if he's lying. A relationship built on a lie that consuming isn't worth a grain of salt."

I make the mistake of catching sight of her face.

"But you're lying to everyone. Wanting them to think I'm your girlfriend when I'm just an accessory to remedy your own adultery train."

"Touché." Twirling the wineglass gives me something to do with my hand. "I never fuck with married women, Magnolia. You should know that."

"How do you know? Everyone lies these days. That's the root of all of this. Goddamn lies." Her chest is rising and falling as her anger takes control of her body. I can't say I blame her. I can't imagine the predicament she's been in. To have her daughter uncover the affair makes it even worse.

I palm my chest. "I don't know. You're right."

"That's all you have to say?" she says, hurt filling her eyes.

The time for running from this fucking mess has passed. I'm invested. My friends call it the hero complex. We make jokes about it. That motherfucking shit is true. I can't turn away from a problem that needs to be solved. I cannot let a beautiful woman like Magnolia flounder like this. It would be criminal if she never pulled herself from this suckfest. Plus, I can confidently say I enjoy talking to her more than I like talking to anyone else.

I scoot my chair back, away from her, giving a polite, neutral distance between our bodies. I nod once. "Tell me everything you're mad about. Let it all out. Everything," I say. She tilts her head, trying to get a read on me and my motives. "Tell me where it hurts. Tell me where the death blow is."

Clasping my hands between my spread knees, I wait.

Her eyes widen and her mouth pops open. She closes it again.

I go on. "When it's all out and there's nothing left to say, it doesn't belong to you anymore. It belongs to me. That's the deal. I'm stealing it."

Magnolia narrows her eyes. "But it won't. It can't. I've lived it. It will always be mine."

I shake my head. "That's the deal. Once you've spoken it, I've taken it from you."

"How much are you paying for my dumpster fire?" She smiles, assuming I'm joking. I look around, wondering how much she leases Magnolia's Steals for. She interrupts my thoughts. "Why in the world would you do anything for me? You barely know me," she says, shakily setting her wineglass down on the desk. "It doesn't make any sense."

"It doesn't have to make sense. I can handle your dumpster fire times a thousand. Give it to me."

She leans forward without realizing she has. Keeping my distance is difficult, the need to comfort her warring with common sense. If I hug her, I'll kiss her, then I'll fuck her on this desk, and she'll still be upset when I leave. If she talks to me about this, there's a chance of her truly getting over the fuckwad, or at least moving on. "Consider it part of the relationship training," I offer, opening my hands and clasping them again. "I'm teaching you how to have a relationship in this century, right?"

She rolls her eyes. "I'm not that out of touch."

"Tell me," I say.

"Where does it hurt?" she asks, wincing. "Everywhere." Magnolia folds her arms around her stomach. "How will I ever trust a man again? How will Kendall move on? A father is supposed to be a role model for their daughter. The type of man they grow up and seek out as a partner." She lays a hand on her forehead. "If he ruined her, I'll kill him. You'll have to do it for me. You protect your kids at all costs, and I couldn't protect her from this."

"Children are resilient," I say, hesitant to give anything that might lead to questions I don't want to answer. "You are a good role model. That's what she needs. She's old enough to realize what he did was wrong. She won't seek out a cheater or a liar. She'll want a real man. She'll be able to sniff out lies better than her peers who haven't had this particular experience. He gave her that gift. The ability to know the difference. Your daughter will get over this. Now, will you? Put her aside for just a second and tell me what you're afraid of outside of parenting and Kendall. Trusting again?" I ask.

Magnolia closes her eyes, and I can see her compartmentalizing. When her gaze meets mine, I see a fire there. "You know when you're young, before you've been burned at all?"

I don't. That was a luxury I wasn't granted, but I nod anyway.

Magnolia goes on, talking with her hands. "Paul was with me since then. There was never a second I didn't trust him. It was always him and me—us. We learned how to be adults together. It was this fragility built from childhood into adulthood. When he cheated," she says, blowing out a breath, "that ruined everything for me. That magic you think is exclusive doesn't exist. It was wiped out with a tsunami of grief."

"You grieve. You move on," I add.

She shakes her head. "I have. I've grieved. How is it fair he gets to have that magic? Without me? We created that together. Does that make sense?"

I clear my throat. Entering awkward territory. "Do you miss him?"

"No. Yes. No. I miss how simple it was when we were together."

"Simple. You used the word 'simple,' Magnolia. True love isn't simple."

"What do you know about true love?"

I look away. More than I should, that's for sure. I'm only in touch with the cruel, masochistic side of love. I know exactly what it's not supposed to be. "This isn't about me. You can have that feeling again. It may not look the same. Or feel the same. It can be different and be just as satisfying. But you don't want different, do you?"

"I want him to suffer like I did."

I correct her. "Like you do. You're obviously suffering now."

She covers her eyes with both palms and rubs back and forth. "That's the thing. I thought I was over him, Aidan. Last night with you. I felt so much. It was an awakening. For stupid news about Paul and Pamela to crash in and ruin everything is devastating. I'm angry he has power over me."

"You're giving it to him."

"You're right," she counters, sighing. "How do I take the power back? Tell me how not to care. I can't feel like this anymore. It's sucking away all my happiness."

"Last night," I say, raising one brow. "How did you feel?"

She opens her eyes wide as she lets memories trickle back in. "There was no pressure. It was easy. I was free." She licks her lips. "I wasn't with you to forget him or get over him. I was merely with you."

"Because it was casual?" I prod.

She looks away. "Because of you." Magnolia shakes her head and looks down.

"What? Tell me."

"You called me your girlfriend in front of Polly, and I hoped you meant it. I know how crazy that is, given we'd only texted a bit and had dinner, but I wanted it to be true. I'm ready for that. I feel like a different person with you. When you just said it can be different but just as satisfying, I knew exactly what you meant. I felt that. I feel like a dope admitting this to you. I barely know you, and you don't know me other than I'm a mess," she continues, slurring her words a bit as she moves her hand up and down her body, attempting to highlight the mess she thinks she is. "I know I don't want Paul." She shakes her head. "I didn't know I could want someone like I want you."

My heart pounds a bit, and it's the first indication that I might feel something that's not altruistic—an actual blossoming of an unrecognizable emotion. "You're not a dope, and I know that you're a brave woman. A strong woman. You've lived through a blow that could take a human down."

She waves around the room. "Is this not me down? Looks like bottom-feeder status to me. Sobbing into a dusty wineglass, whining to a stranger about my ex-husband."

I shake my head. "You're strong when it matters. Everyone reaches a breaking point. And I'm not a stranger, Magnolia. I can still taste you. We are far from strangers."

A blush creeps up her cheeks. "I do feel better now."

"Because you got it all off your chest?" I ask.

"No. Because you cared enough to stay and listen."

My throat clogs with emotion. "I've taken Paul from you," I say, clearing my throat halfway through my sentence. "That fucker is owned by Aidan Mixx. You understand?"

"For what price?"

"My manhood," I counter, grinning. The big one I know she'll respond to.

Her tongue flicks out to wet her lips. Perfection.

"Manhood?" she asks, voice low.

"Will you be my real girlfriend, Magnolia Sager? Not for pretend to get the chicks off my jock, but because I like you. I like that you're complex—that you tell me what's on your mind even if it might make me uncomfortable. I like that you put your daughter first. I like that you want magic after being hurt. I like that you're good." I shake my head. "I'm not going to let anyone else ruin you, and you're not going to fix me," I deadpan. "Let me try to fix you, and maybe your magic will rub off on me."

Her full, wet lips open a touch to expose her white teeth. "I'm drunk, but you're serious right now, aren't you? This is real life?"

"You're a cheap date," I say. "I'm nothing if not serious."

Magnolia stands from her stool and crooks her finger at me. "I'd sit on your lap right now, but we'd break that chair. It's a mid-century Bentwood."

Standing slowly, I let out a deep breath to clear my head and the nervous energy in the air. "You're so hot when you talk antique to me," I drawl, stepping closer to wrap an arm around her waist and pull her against my body. She's warm, and her reaction to my touch is immediate. Her flesh bristles and her breath catches. "Tell me more," I rasp, my cock straining against my jeans.

She goes on her tiptoes and presses her lips up to meet mine. I groan when the first taste hits my senses. Relief. Sweet, blissful relief. I've craved this in unquantifiable amounts. Her lips smack as she pulls away to say, "One owner. Nice patina. 1940s. Maybe '30s."

"Fuck yes," I growl, taking her lips again. I get carried away easily—lifting her body to set her on the desk. Her legs wrap around my waist, and I'm hit with the frantic need to be inside her. There's a desperation I've felt only a couple of times before. Once was when I returned home from a year-long deployment. A year without sex. It was the longest I'd ever gone, and my brain crossed so many wires I wasn't sure where to begin when I had a woman in my bed the day after I got back in the States. I had to hold back the urge to go caveman on her and fuck a hole in the mattress. The sex ended with me having a girlfriend. It was as if I'd tricked myself into thinking the sex was something special when really it was my first wet pussy in a long-ass time. The woman was a narcissist—an opportunist. I figured it out eventually, but not before I gave a little more than I wanted to.

Right now, with Magnolia, the desperation is in opposition to that relationship. It's a need to show her that I can fuck Paul away. That I can give her more than he can. I'll make her crazy. Prove that her ex is a bad memory that isn't worth being haunted over. I'll make sure she knows I'm capable of being the man she needs. Does it appeal to my need for a challenge? Yes. It doesn't change the fact everything I said to her is truth. I do like her. I want her.

"Is this going down right here?" I ask. "The chair is safe, but I might break the desk." My lips are speaking against her mouth, but she's watching my eyes. "Where can I make love to you?"

Her breath catches, and her arms slide from around my head to push against my chest. I think I'm being shot down completely until she smirks and takes my hand. "Come with me."

"I hope to," I say, letting her guide me out of the room.

SIX

Magnolia

The old wooden stairs creak loudly as Aidan's large frame weighs on each step. "It's hot up here," I say as we reach the top landing and the humidity hits us like a right hook. "But I know I have a fan in here somewhere." Reaching into a coat closet, I pull out a fan. Aidan takes it from me and waits for me to direct him where to go. We enter a room across the hall. I use it for storage, but there is a bed. Rephrase that: there is a bed frame and a mattress standing against a wall.

I wince when I see the state of the room. "Sort of looks like a room used for prostitution. Or a squatter's residence. Or something really seedy and related to a trap house. If you want to go to your place, we can," I offer, fumbling for the correct words. He's being so understanding about everything, and I feel like the weak link who can't get anything right. "It is really hot," I repeat.

Tell me where it hurts. A phrase I've said to Kendall a thousand times. You say those words when you care so much that you'd do anything, anything in the world to ease the pain from the place it exudes from. Surely the words don't mean the same thing when Aiden says them. Do they? "And it's not romantic in any way," I add, wondering if I've gone absolutely crazy.

"Stop," Aidan says. "Move out of the way."

I do as he says, the feral look in his eyes not to be challenged for fear of it diminishing even a minuscule amount. He wants me, and I can hear it in every word he says, in every move he makes. I back into the doorway, out of his way, as he plugs in the fan and turns it on high. He grabs the mattress and tilts it so it falls directly on the wooden frame.

"I've been meaning to get this to my house for the spare room but didn't want to ask for help getting it down the stairs and into my truck," I explain.

Hands on his hips, he surveys the bed, then turns to look at me over his shoulder. "Tell you what, once I've fucked you on it, I'll put it in your truck. How's that sound?"

I swallow down the huge ball of anxious nerves. He has turned my jagged cry fest into a sexual tension so great I can barely stand still without vibrating out of my clothing. Aidan pulls on the back collar of his shirt and slides it off. He's sweating—beads of sweat sliding down his neck, sluicing down his chest and abs. My mouth waters.

Aidan watches me watching him, his smug grin fading into something more serious. "This isn't rebound fucking, Magnolia. Do you understand? You have to look me in the eye tomorrow and not feel embarrassed about everything you confessed tonight. This isn't casual anymore."

I wasn't planning on ghosting him, but now that he's mentioned it, maybe I was. I slide my shorts off and strip off my tank top. "Isn't that my line?" I ask, unfastening my bra and tossing the sweaty fabric aside.

"Leave the panties on," Aidan barks when I tuck my thumbs into them. "Those are mine to take off."

They are black lace, different than last night, but still just as amazing. I had some intuition to wear decent undergarments when I got out of the shower in a haze of emotions this morning. I nod. "I'm going to look you in the eye tomorrow. This isn't me rebound fucking,"

Aidan says, shaking his head once. "We clear?"

My stomach flips. His maleness is prominent—his needs on display. His heart on his sleeve. "You wouldn't be a rebound even if that was my plan, Aidan. You're too good at giving me orgasms. I'll always want more from you. I'm afraid that you're going to tire of me after."

Aidan fishes a condom out of his pocket, tosses it on the bed, and steps out of his jeans. His dick springs free, and I lose my breath at the magnificent specimen in front of me. "It's fine if I hook you with my bedroom skills, but I want you to stay."

He wraps a hand around his hard-on, and the sight of his fingers gripping the girth-laden shaft makes my head swim and my knees weak. I wasn't granted this view last night, no. It was all about me and my pleasure. Aidan played my body with deft hands and a skilled tongue. His words praised me just as much as his body did.

Even right now he's saying all of the right things, but Aidan isn't making me forget Paul. He's erasing him completely by being everything he never was. Aidan is different. He crooks his finger, the same way I did to him earlier. I close the distance between us as more sweat beads on his shoulders and neck.

"You're hot," I say.

"You are making me hot, Magnolia," he says, taking my panties in his big hands and ripping them off. "Not the weather."

I gasp from the shock of the force but settle into full-fledged passion a moment later, consumed by how frenzied he is with feeling my body—his palms grazing my breasts and shoulders, sliding a bit because a sheen of sweat glazes my entire body. It's not uncomfortable heat, just enough to make me self-aware of every breath, every beautiful drop of wetness on his muscles, bringing out the scent of masculinity—of Aidan.

He takes my chin in his hand and jerks it up so I'm gazing into his hazel eyes. "You're perfect," he says. And even though I'm not, I believe it when he says it. "Kiss me."

Throwing my arms around his neck, I bring our warm bodies together and obey his command. It's a desolate kiss that ends with me on top of him on the bare mattress. There is a desperation in the way his fingers glide over my skin, the way he breathes rapidly, and the flex of his abs as he exerts self-control in a scene that reeks of two people who have no control whatsoever.

I trail my hands over his muscles, memorizing the feel—the curve, the hardness. "Aidan," I say, speaking the word into his open mouth while catching my breath. I remember what he told me about letting go—being in the moment and feeling it—so that's what I do. I close my eyes as he reaches between my legs and strokes me with deft, experienced fingers. I slide off his sweaty body a bit and have to reposition myself to gain purchase.

"Does that feel good?" he asks, taking my earlobe into his mouth. He sucks once or twice and releases it, creating chills despite the warmth at all angles. "I want to make you feel good."

I'd respond if I wasn't on the brink of orgasm—I'd tell him being this close to his body gives me life, passion, a whole new destiny, but I keep that vested in favor of moaning for him to press harder. I open my eyes before I come, and he's watching our entwined bodies in an old mirror that covers almost the entire wall next to us.

"Watch me," he commands. "The mirror. Watch us." With my hands sliding on his chest, he lifts me up farther on my knees and pushes me back as he handles his dick. He grabs the condom next to us, rips it open, and slides it over his shaft while looking directly at me.

I watch the hazy reflection as he slides me forward and positions himself, tilts his hips up so just the tip enters my body, and then turns his head to the side to meet my gaze in the mirror. "Are you watching?" he asks, eyes flickering with an emotion I don't fully understand.

I'm transfixed. It's as if I'm watching two other people in the throes of passion, yet my body is on fire. "I can't look away," I confess.

His smile at my words is lackadaisical at best. "Ride me," he returns, setting his hands on my hips, a light touch. "Like you mean it."

He was all business while we were talking downstairs, straightforward and practical. The man in the mirror doesn't even seem like the same person. The man beneath me, the one who is currently entering my body as I slide down, inch by inch, is someone else entirely. An entity granted for my pleasure—the man is made for this. I wanted this last night more than I care to admit, but now I'm glad I had a warm-up.

The slick feel of his hands on me guide me to a pleasurable pace—one that makes him groan, and my eyes roll back in my head. Feeling him fill my body is sensational, the connection unlike anything I have ever felt. I watch him in the mirror while he watches me in real time, his eyes narrowed, his bottom lip caught between his teeth.

He lets me ride him up and down a few more times, muscles coiled in restraint, and then he slides me off him and lays me back on the mattress, parting my legs with one of his knees. Aidan settles between my legs, thrusting into me in one, core-clenching push. "That feels good," I cry, tipping my chin up to receive his fiery lips. Sweat, his and mine, mingles, creating a slippery friction that lights the air with the scent of sex. Leaning away from our kiss, he buries his face in my neck and breathes heavy, his free hand wrapped around the base of my neck, a reminder who is running things right now.

"You're so fucking tight," he rasps. "This is mine." Aidan swallows audibly and thrusts deep inside me, rubbing me in all the right places. The frame of the bed squeaks out in protest as he ravages me—brings me closer to blissed-out paradise.

"It's yours," I repeat, jagged breaths catching my words. "I'm almost there." Tilting my hips up, I slide my hand between our wet bodies and stroke my clit as the pleasure builds. Aidan keeps the pace the same, his breathing uneven, his hand skimming the side of my body to end under my thigh.

He pulls my leg up to fuck me at a deeper angle and I come apart, one wave of pleasure at a time. I can feel his smile against my neck as he stays deep inside me as my orgasm hits. Closing my eyes against the onslaught of feelings, I ride it all the way up and back down. My heart is beating out of my chest, a reminder that I am in fact living in this moment instead of dreaming of it. A string of curse words exits my mouth when I finally have my wits enough to speak.

Aidan juts his hips when my body relaxes into the afterglow, and he comes in a rapid fierceness so strong I can feel his orgasm pulse against my channel. He grunts, relaxes with his elbows on either side of me and slides his forehead over to rest on top of mine. Sweat. So much sweat is glistening on our bodies. I don't know which is his or which is mine.

"That was the hottest sex I've ever had," he says, taking my bottom lip in between his teeth. "In both temperature and physically," he explains.

I smile with my eyes, unable to move my mouth. He releases my mouth with a kiss. "Is that a bad thing?" I ask, floating around in that after sex cloud of delirium laced with lust-tainted love. Casual, I remind myself. Even if I am his girlfriend, this is casual sex. *Don't make a big deal about it. Don't show him too much. You showed too much downstairs. Keep this close.*

"It's a very good thing, Magnolia," Aidan chirps, a wide, lazy smile on his face. It steals my breath when he says my name paired with that smile. He reaches between our bodies and pulls the condom off. He ties it, hunts for the wrapper, and slides the cum-filled latex into the foil.

"I've never had sex with a condom before," I

admit. So much for not giving him anything else. "It feels…different."

Aidan grins. "Does it? I've never had sex without one."

I must look shocked because he goes on. "Not a risk I'd ever take."

"Oh," I reply, sitting up, dabbing sweat off my chin. "Even if you were exclusive with someone?" I eye the foil and raise a brow. "Seems a little unnecessary if other measures were in place."

"I control a condom. I can't control a chick taking a pill at the same time every day," he says, glancing away. I prod a bit more, and he tells me he's not opposed to having children eventually, but he wants them to be planned. He's not good with surprises.

Swallowing, I come to my knees and press my body against his. "That was amazing. The best sex of my life. I just can't help but wonder what it might feel like to have you inside me without barriers—with nothing between us. Just skin. You and I."

Aidan's neck works. "When you put it like that," he says, chuckling. Aidan explains how he gets tested at work monthly for STDs or any sort of health ailments, really, and then I tell him how I have a nifty IUD that prevents pregnancy. He seems intrigued, almost as if I'm an alien when I tell him how it works. "You mean there's fishing wire in there, and I didn't feel it?"

I nod. "And it stays in place for fifteen years. I had it put in years ago and didn't bother having it taken out after the divorce. It seemed easier to leave it there."

"You've given me something to think about."

"I can't believe you've never considered it in the past. You've been in relationships."

He clears his throat, pressing a kiss to the side of my head. "They weren't the trustworthy kind."

"I am?" I ask, grinning. I can feel his erection rising again.

Aidan shifts so it's between my legs, the warmth pressing at my core but not entering. His breath hitches. "You are, I think. Even if I rarely trust anyone."

"Why?" I ask.

"Because you trusted me with your truths," he replies, pulling away to look me in the eye. "You feel better now, don't you?"

My stomach flips as I look into his eyes. "I don't even remember where it hurts anymore."

Aidan smiles. "We'll have to repeat your pain management treatments daily."

Licking my lips, I say, "Thank you. I don't think you realize how much tonight has meant to me."

Eyes narrowed, he studies me, like he's trying to fish a lie. A rash of unwarranted self-conscious nerves winds around me. "You're the one taking a chance on a bad boy," Aidan says, cocking his head to the side and cupping my face in his big hands. Hazel eyes dip down, and a haunting glow replaces the sweet one. "You hold all the risk."

"I also hold all of the reward then," I reply, pressing my lips together.

"Fuck, Magnolia," Aidan hisses before pulling my mouth to his. "I want all of you."

There has never been anything easier than living, and feeling in this moment.

Nothing.

SEVEN
Aidan

"You can't fucking talk like that when she gets here, bro," I rasp at my friend after he used several four-letter words to describe his most recent hookup. He's tending the grill, flipping burgers with the precision of a surgeon. "She'll be here in ten minutes, and I'm about to shit my pants."

I have never, not once, been in the scenario where I'm introducing a woman to my friends, the SEALs who I share everything with. It's scary and disconcerting, and it feels like I'm turning a corner at a million miles per hour when I wasn't planning on taking that turn. It can't be bad. This has to be moving forward, the progression of two people who get along and want to spend time together. The reason I didn't introduce the women from my past to my brothers is because I didn't trust the chicks enough not to jump into bed with my teammates.

Maybe it's a case of low self-esteem, maybe it's the product of selecting horrible women to spend my time with. All I know right now is that Magnolia is different. She won't want to fuck my friends, but my friends might fuck me by saying something stupid. I want to protect Magnolia. From her past. From brutal words that can be avoided. I want to protect her from everything I can. She's been through so much.

"Don't shit your pants. I won't say anything," Mercer drawls, his southern accent strong. Mercer is a good ole boy through and through. As testament, he is wearing a pair of worn-in cowboy boots with black board shorts. The entirety of his massive upper body is covered in dark blue ink. My name is in there somewhere, as are a few other teammates who were on a particular mission where he almost lost his life. Narrowing my eyes, I locate my name, right next to a big fat zit on a pinup girl's forehead. Sighing, I shake my head. Mercer.

He waves the spatula in his hand like it's a fairy wand or some shit and spits into a brown-tinged Pepsi bottle. "You're so magical now. A girlfriend. That's some unbelievable shit. I can't take your word for it. I need to hear it from her mouth. You understand my reasons."

I grunt in response and restack the bags of buns on top of the plates.

Every once in a while, we'll grill out at the beach on our base. The group gets a little smaller with each passing month. When my brothers get girlfriends, they have better things to do than shoot the shit at work in their free time. Tahoe and Leif, my two best friends, are home with their women. I'm trying to prove that even if I add a woman to my life, I can still hang. Nothing will change. I won't let it.

When Mercer starts dancing, gyrating his pelvis in

my direction while singing a made-up song about my dick and manhood, I wave him off.

I grab two beers from the large stainless-steel cooler and walk down to the hard-packed beach sand. Tahoe built a few picnic tables that we drag out of a storage shed for occasions such as this. I sit at the one that's empty and contemplate every single decision that led to this night. It's odd—a shock to everyone who knows me.

Colton, a SEAL who was recently transferred to Bronze Bay from Harbour Point, our base in Cape Cod, collapses onto the table in front of me. "I'm feeling so emo these days. It's the heat. I'm never going to get used to it. Thank God we don't actually work here."

"Your flair for dramatics is impressive. You get used to the heat," I reply, smirking. Magnolia's naked, sweaty body comes to mind, and I have to control my wild thoughts. "There are tradeoffs. Jaws isn't prowling here."

"The sharks never fuck with us," he counters. "The chicks are hot here, but I miss the northern weather. I was in San Diego before Harbour Point, remember that. The sun is manic here," Colton says, moaning. He's shirtless, wearing a pair of black issued workout shorts that hit thigh-high. The sun is already set, and he's still complaining. It's amusing. "Is dinner almost ready?"

"Yes, darling. It's almost ready," I coo in a sarcastic voice. "Are you going out after we eat?" I ask, curious if they are prowling tonight like I used to. It's not jealousy that drives the question because the mere thought of the work that goes into hooking up for one night and ditching them is pretty extensive.

There's always the risk of a stage one clinger, like Wildcat.

Colton sits up and rests on his elbows. "I don't know. It's so hot. I might just go home and turn the A/C as high as it will go and see if I can break the unit. That sounds like a good time, doesn't it?"

"No," I deadpan. "It doesn't. But you've always been a bit of a pussy, so it doesn't surprise me."

"Fuck you, man. Speaking of, aren't you the one banging the same pussy every night?"

I scoff. "No." The lie came without my permission.

"No?" Colton quirks a brow and then aims his gaze up toward base. I turn my head and glimpse Magnolia standing in a group of guys. There are a couple of other women mixed in, but it's primarily my teammates. Slamming the rest of my beer, I jump up and jog to the powwow just in time to hear Mercer's high-pitched chuckle.

"And that's when I knew there was no other job for me," Mercer finishes, flexing his bicep in an over-exaggerated way.

I roll my eyes and groan. "Is this buffoon bothering you?" I ask, snaking an arm around Magnolia, claiming her.

Her eyes light when mine meet hers. The crackle of sexual tension buzzes where my clothed body presses against hers.

"No, he was just explaining the finer nuances of grilling," Magnolia says, smiling wide. "I think?"

Glaring at Mercer, I thump him on the shoulder harder than a friendly tap.

"Hey man, you weren't here to greet your woman, so I did it for you. It was a pleasure to meet you, Magnolia Sager. I look forward to visiting your shop soon." Mercer bows, putting the spatula against his chest.

"He's not right in the head. Too many explosions," I counter. "Let me properly introduce you to everyone," I say, my words clogging in my throat. Am I doing it right? Can she tell I don't know what the fuck I'm doing—mixing two worlds without an instruction manual?

"Calm down," Magnolia whispers as I guide her by her elbow away from the crowd. "I'm here for a cheeseburger, Aidan."

Closing my eyes, I sigh. "You're right. I'm sorry. I don't know what's wrong with me. This isn't a big deal."

"It's really not. Normal, average people do this sort of thing all the time. Introducing one friend to another. It's casual," Magnolia says, squeezing my hand in hers. "You like that word, right?"

When we're far enough away, I spin her toward me. "There's nothing normal about me. Or average about you. There's nothing casual about us. I've never done this before," I admit, trying to control my heart rate. "I don't have family. This is the equivalent of you meeting my mother."

Magnolia laughs, her bright white smile melting away any residual fears that linger. "I'm honored to meet your mother. Even if she's a beastly six-foot-four shirtless creature who wears boots to the beach. It's a bit odd, but you know, I can't judge."

"Mercer is a little much. It would have been better if we started introductions with the tamer variety." I see a few who meet that criteria and flag them over. I introduce Magnolia to them, and they are gracious, and for reasons I can't fathom, they don't try to fuck me over. They only say good things about me and talk me up. Magnolia is animated as she asks questions about their lives and our chosen career. They answer, and one by one, I see the spark, the glamour in their eyes as they see what I do—recognize Magnolia for what she is and mostly for what she is not.

She's safe enough enveloped in Colton's rant about humidity and sweat, so I grab a couple burgers from the grill, tuck beers under my arms, and find an empty spot at a picnic table. I fix the burgers, trying to sort what I think Magnolia would like on her burger. In the end, I fix it the same as mine: all the way.

I'm walking over to tell her it's ready, but Leo stops me, a tight hand on my arm. "I got second dibs," he says, eyes never leaving Magnolia. The nefarious flicker warns me he's serious.

"Fuck you, Leo. This is a no-dibs thing. She is not the kind of woman we normally hang out with. You know that, though, or you wouldn't be interested." It's a new relationship, so my single friends will test the boundaries. Will we take sloppy seconds in a different scenario? Sure. If it's a one-night stand, chances are we've double-dipped unaware. "Stay away from her," I say, driving my point home. "Magnolia is off-limits."

"Is she?" Leo smirks, and my stomach coils. Why do I care that he's being a smarmy bastard? I've been the same smarmy bastard in the past when I was younger. I get it now—how a woman, the right woman, can change almost everything in the blink of an eye. Leo is heading to Harbour Point soon. He was a trade for Colton to keep the bases evenly staffed. He's from Cape Cod and has been trying to work his way back there since he recently graduated BUD/S. He is a fresh nineteen-year-old and doesn't have any limits—a mere child in the arena of seasoned pros. If our current conversation has anything to say about his maturity level, he has much to learn. And he will probably learn it the hard way.

"Leo. I'm fucking serious," I growl under my breath when I see Magnolia peering around Colton's shoulder to catch my eye. "Stay the fuck away from Magnolia."

"I will stay the fuck away from Magnolia," he says, repeating my words back to me, slithering away, back to the shadows he crept from.

My skin prickles, and I fucking hate the feeling. Throwing up a hand, I hike my thumb over my shoulder at the table. Magnolia excuses herself from Colton's whining tirade and approaches. Her tank top is tight, and her shorts are short. The light from the scattered tiki torches lends just enough to make her glow. As she walks toward me, she looks like an angel, one that every other man here is watching in this moment. Her smile is only for me, her gaze all fucking mine, and all hesitations melt away. Her gait pauses when she's standing in front of me.

"Burgers ready?" she asks, licking her lips.

I take her face in my hands, a tender gesture I'd second-guess any other time given the circumstances, and I shock all of these bastards when I lean in and kiss Magnolia with pent-up passion. She folds into me, pressing her body against mine, her chin tipped up to take anything I'll give her.

When I pull away from the kiss, her eyes look glazed over. She's turned on, and my pulse ratchets up in response. I keep my hand on her face and say, "Burgers are ready, but more importantly, you are so fucking beautiful."

She swallows hard. "You're making me blush."

"You're making me crazy," I counter, grinning.

"I've missed you," she says, keeping her voice low. She senses all of the eyes and ears on us. "Maybe we can get out of here after we eat?" she says. "I only have a couple hours. Kendall is at a fundraiser meeting at the high school. I need to pick her up in a bit."

I nod. I get it now. Why Tahoe and Leif aren't here. How the world shifts, tilts, in favor of the person who grants you the most happiness. "Let's eat, my place after."

Magnolia comments on how good the cheeseburger is, and I mentally pat myself on the back for my choice in condiments. She asks me questions about the guys in between bites, but we put the burgers and beer down in record time.

"Now is the time when we either pop smoke or start telling everyone goodbye," Magnolia says. "Creep out, or make a show of it? I want them to like me, so maybe we say bye." She tosses the options back and forth in her mind, and I see her balancing the pros and cons of each. When her gaze lights on mine, she knows what I'm thinking, and that makes her decision easy.

"We can go up the dock on the other side. There aren't torches over there, so it will be dark. You up for an adventure?" I say, nuzzling her ear with my nose. She leans into my face, and I kiss her neck. Her lavender perfume mixed with sweat. It might as well be toxic. My mouth waters.

"I'll never say no to adventure," she counters. "Especially with you."

After I toss our garbage in the big can, I return to Magnolia and grab her hand. When we're far enough away, and the blackness takes over our sight, I pull her up onto my back. She giggles and tightens her grip around my neck.

The waves roll against the shore softly—a lulling sound as opposed to the angry Pacific Ocean break. The moon lights the way as I listen to Magnolia breathe gently by my ear. It's a peace I am not used to knowing. Sure, there are moments of still silence, moments I reflect about how far I've come, but peace hasn't ever been mine. There's always, in some form or another, a shouting of protest—a war of unease that beats at my chest, a wrongly accused prisoner begging to be set free.

The light post beckons our arrival, but I need to tell Magnolia I want to stay out here in the blackness, with her heartbeat, a little longer. Feel this unknown peace, taste it, familiarize myself with it. "It's such a nice night," Magnolia whispers into my ear. "Do you see the moon?"

My heart stops beating for a moment, and she feels it, too. She must. I let her slide off my back and bring her back against my front as we sit in the sand. A contented sigh escapes her lips, and I do my best to rein in my emotions. "It's almost a full moon," I reply. "There is a tiny sliver missing."

"I don't know," Magnolia returns. "It looks full to me."

She doesn't know what she's stirring, what she's fixing, or how she's forming a person who has never really existed before this very moment.

"Get your ass off the bed, you weak little fucker," he roars.

I cover my ears because it hurts me. The words and the tone. My stomach hurts as I scramble off the bed in a sleepy haze and retreat under the wooden table in the corner of my bedroom. It's the furthest point from my bedroom door, where he's standing in blackness.

"So-so-sorry, Daddy," I stammer, wrapping my arms around my knees, the cold wall stinging my bare skin. He fell asleep, and my back was hurting while I slept on the floor. I thought I could sneak into the bed without him knowing. I'd be back on the floor before he woke in the morning. The trick has worked in the past. "I'm sorry. I'll stay here. Please."

I plead with him even though I know he's going to beat me. It will only hurt for a few hours, and I'll try not to make the same mistake again. It's hard to remember what he doesn't like me to do. There are so many things. Mommy is already sleeping. She sleeps a lot. Most of the day and all night long. I get to see her after school on occasion. Sometimes she'll even smile at me and pat my head. She kissed my cheek on my birthday last year, maybe she'll kiss me again soon.

Daddy beats me, pulls my pants down, and uses the thick, black belt. He misses my behind, and the crack stings my back. I think of her kiss, though. It keeps me from crying. Daddy doesn't like tears either. "Tears are weak," he says. Sleeping in beds makes me weak. I need to be a man. A strong man. He leaves the bed in my room as a temptation, he says. So I can control myself and make the right choices. I want to be a strong man. A big man. I want Mommy's kisses. I sleep on the floor.

A tear sneaks out when the lash hits my side instead of my back. It hurts the worst when he misses and gets the tender skin. The teardrop hits the tile floor, and I close my eyes so no more tears will come out. Daddy will be mad. Tears are for girls. For people who can't control their emotions. Mommy never comes in. I think that's why Daddy is so mad. I don't want him to hit her, though. I'd rather he hit me because I can handle it. She can't. She's too tired. I'm a man.

He screams at me now that he's finished with the belt. I can tell when he's done because he's out of breath and his arm shakes. "You are a pathetic excuse for a son. Do you hear me? You are a weak son of a bitch who will never be a fucking man. I'll never be able to make you a fucking man if you don't obey me, you little fuck. Do you understand me, Aidan? I'm doing this to make you a better man."

I stand, but my legs are shaky, and my skin feels like fire. "Yes, sir," I say, keeping my voice loud and proud, like a strong man. "It won't happen again."

"You say that, and yet it does. Time and again. Can you not handle the temptation? Are you that weak?" he asks.

I shake my head.

"Answer me verbally, you little pussy."

"No, sir," I say, getting angry with myself for forgetting. Again. Maybe I'll never be a strong man. I can't remember. I close my eyes and tick through all of the things that will make me a man. I want my mommy's kiss. I can't stop thinking about it.

"Lie down," he yells. I flinch but pretend it is part of the motion of hitting the floor. I tuck my head on my hands and slam my eyes shut. Daddy leaves, but he's still here. All over my skin. I sniffle once, and tears leak out onto the tile—my tile bed.

Mommy.

Mommy.

I want you.

Mommy.

Kisses.

Save me.

EIGHT

Magnolia

I PICKED up Kendall from the high school, and now I'm sitting at the kitchen table, swirling a glass of red wine while Jenny gives me the latest gossip. "Did you know it was three guys, not two? He didn't even know until after the divorce." Jenny's playing her favorite game of seek and tell.

"I think something is up with Aidan," I butt in, changing the direction of our conversation completely. "Before you say I told you so, I want you to know that's not what I mean. Like, we could have had dirty, furious sex at his house, and instead we ended up sitting at the beach talking. For an hour. He held me in his arms."

"Whoa, like you think this might be super real, like legit, put a ring on it, super real?" Jenny asks, draining her wine.

Kendall and Juliet filter into the room for their popcorn that just finished popping, talking about some sort of ponytail holder they saw on Instagram. Jenny and I stay silent, waiting for them to disperse. I haven't been completely honest with her about my feelings for

Aidan. Until recently, I wasn't honest with myself about my feelings for Aidan. Now, not only am I confident I'm falling for him, I think the falling might have already happened.

"Super, legit real, Jenny. I wasn't expecting anything more than maybe exclusive casual dating, but he seems to be all in. It's hard to be sure because it's just been Paul for me, but I don't think I've ever felt like this before," I say, tilting my wineglass to watch the wine dance around, my mind spinning future possibilities that make me giddy. "I told you about the night at Magnolia's Steals, how he talked to me about the affair, and Paul, and everything."

"And the wild, hot sex you had after," Jenny adds, hissing it under her breath. "You told me."

I hold my pointer finger against my lips. "Keep your voice down. I haven't told Kendall anything. And I definitely don't want those images in her head."

Jenny widens her eyes. "You can't fall in love without telling her, Magnolia. Give the kid a heads-up before a new daddy waltzes in and rocks her world. She's almost an adult. I think with the history with Paul, you need to be completely honest with her. What if she freaks out? You told her you were dating, right?"

Kind of. In really loose terms I wasn't sure she'd understand.

"Yeah, I told her you wanted me to go on coffee dates and, like, make friends with men and women my age to expand my horizons."

Jenny shakes her head, her lips pressed into a duckbill. "You need to come clean."

"I don't want her to think she won't be my number one priority, you know? Will she feel abandoned? I don't think bringing another man into her life is smart. Why not wait until she's moved out?"

Jenny snarls, "Please tell me your plan for this then? Keep the man a secret until she goes to college and then say *surprise, here's your new daddy*!"

I shrug. "That is a horrible idea," she continues. "An idea I doubt Aidan would agree to anyway. Does he not want to meet her?"

I think about what he said tonight, about how I was essentially meeting his family by meeting his SEAL teammates, and the guilt hits me square in the chest. "This is different. It's tricky with Kendall. She's still so sensitive. I'd cut it off now if I could, but I think I'm in too deep."

Jenny smiles. "This is rich, Magnolia. You are so in love with this bad boy. At least introduce me to him." She pours herself more wine, her third glass.

"You staying over tonight then?" I tease.

"I wasn't planning on it, but this is too good. Drink up. We have things to discuss."

Shaking my head, I smile. "Want to meet him? Maybe we can meet for dinner this week. I can have him bring a friend." I waggle my brows.

"Hell to the no. Don't entangle me in this testosterone-induced mess. I have a date with Harry, the plumber, on Friday. He's a nice, stable man. Doesn't even have kids!"

I snort. "Fine. Fine. I just can't describe what I felt tonight," I say, floating back to the beach, his arms wrapped around me. For a few moments, I forget the world existed outside of our moment. It was ethereal. The moon, the waves. The sound of his voice. The beats of his heart against my back, a steady symphony.

"Sounds like falling in love," Jenny says, taking a sip, eyeing me over the rim.

"I'd challenge that, but I'm not sure you're wrong. It never felt like this with Paul. It always just was. This is different. I feel like it's a story I'm actually a part of, not one that was predestined because of the circumstances. It's mine. Ours."

"God, that's deep, Magnolia. I might want a piece of this, after all. Are all of his friends whores too?"

Rolling my eyes, I remember meeting them earlier. "Kind of. Some ooze whore more than others. They're also good at trying not to ooze whore, so it could be an act. I think you have to get to know them first, and you can gauge for yourself." Jenny is a beautiful woman, but like me, she's been single for a long time. The difference is, she'll go on a date every once in a while. The dates never escalate into anything else, and then she begins back at square one. She calls it harmless hunting.

"Mom." Kendall pops her head into the room. "Can we go down to the beach? Sandy Beach," she says, clarifying. It's right down the path, past the docks a bit. It's small, but sometimes there are parties there.

"It's late, honey. Why didn't you go earlier?" I ask.

Juliet pops her head in. "Come on, Mom. Just a quick bike ride, and we'll be back before eleven."

"What's down there?" I ask.

Jenny clears her throat. "Who is down there?"

"A few of the girls on the cheer squad," Juliet explains. "They're just hanging out."

"Hanging out is code for underage drinking and boys," I interrupt. Jenny punches a fist in the air in agreement. "I'll keep the tracker on your phone if I agree," I say.

"That's fine. Keep the tracker on. That's where we're going. I wouldn't lie to you, Mom. No boys or alcohol. I promise."

In an effort to give her a tiny bit of freedom, I make my decision. I glance at Jenny and can tell she's arrived at the same decision I have.

"Be back in an hour. Make sure the batteries on your bike lights are fully charged."

"Yes," Kendall squeals loudly, clapping her hands. "A nighttime bike ride is going to be so fun!" Kendall runs over and kisses my cheek as Juliet hugs her mom and they bound out the back door.

"It's safe, right?" Jenny asks.

"It's less than half a mile," I counter. "They're going to be in college all on their own before we know it."

"It's late," she says.

I shrug. "They are teens. This is teen stuff." I pull my phone out of my purse hanging over the chair next to me and pull up the family tracking app. "We'll watch them ride there and back."

"And while they are there?" Jenny says.

"We trust them to use decent judgment," I reply. I don't say good judgment, I say decent. Good comes later, when you've been burned a few times and can rationalize. Decent won't get you pregnant. My stomach sours at the thought.

"Maybe Kendall will use the same judgment as her mom," Jenny quips as if reading my mind.

"Ha. Ha. You're an awful friend," I say, rising from my chair, cell in hand. "Want to help me make a board? You cut the cheese, I'll find crackers." Jenny agrees, her excitement for food paired with her wine, effervescent. We chat about mundane things while we eat, both of us watching the Kendall dot arrive at the beach.

"Technology really is a beautiful thing," Jenny says, stuffing her face with a cracker. "What did we do without it?"

I can't remember. It's been that long, and that's embarrassing given what I do for a living. I offer a weak joke about being old and continue my cell phone stare down. Trust. I need to trust her. If I give her trust, she'll return it and maybe I can be honest about Aidan and my feelings for him. Or maybe I wait a few more months to see how things unfold, and if things blossom like I'm positive they will, then I'll tackle that conversation. I'm giving myself easy outs. It's disconcerting.

Jenny's brutal question brings me to the present. "Did you call Paul about the wedding yet?"

I exhale deeply. "I should do it now," I reply. "I didn't want to be wrapped up in my own emotions when I called. That's not fair. It's hard being diplomatic when I want to call and scream at him like a rabid bear." I focus on my breathing.

"Call him now. I want to hear," Jenny says, eyes widening.

"You are such a gossipmonger. You know you can't tell anyone, right? This is my business, and I don't want Bronze Bay talking about my life."

"That's offensive. You're my best friend. It won't leave the room."

I set a hand on her shoulder. "My best friend who likes gossip. Give me your phone," I say, holding out my hand. "Watch the Kendall and Juliet dot while I call Paul."

She claps giddily and hands over her phone. I don't

need a reference to remember Paul's cell phone number. He hasn't changed it, and right now I wish he had—wish I had to look it up instead of recalling it by memory. Swallowing hard, I hit call and wait. He answers on the first ring, with an uneasy, questioning tone.

"Hey Paul, it's me," I reply.

"Hey Maggie," he says. I cringe but don't correct him because it's not worth it, not when I have bigger fish to fry.

Clearing my throat, I focus on the end goal and what I want out of this call. "Kendall isn't comfortable going to your wedding."

"Goddammit, why can't you talk to her? Tell her I'm not a bad guy?" His reply is hissed, and that only serves to stoke my fury.

"Listen, Paul, I don't tell her how to feel. Despite what you might think, she's almost an adult, more mature than her peers because of what she's been through…what she's seen," I sling, hoping to hit him where it hurts. "She makes her own decisions. I told her to call and apologize for the mean things she said about *her*. I parent her. I don't tell her how to think."

"Pamela. Her name is Pamela. Come on, at least dignify the woman who will be Kendall's stepmother by calling her by her name." My whole body heats at the insinuation of that woman being any relation to my daughter. She *almost* single-handedly destroyed the innocence of my child.

"I tried being nice, but Kendall will never refer to that woman as her stepmother. You ruined that chance when you fucked her on our dining room table knowing we were both in the house. Now before you think I'm holding some grudge, I want you to know

I've moved on. Kendall won't see me fucking him, Paul. She won't. Because I'm an adult, and I handle my relationships, all of them, with dignity and truth. I called to tell you Kendall will not attend your wedding. I called to tell you that you're an asshole to think she would. I called to thank you for being a cheating bastard. If you hadn't, I might still be trapped in a loveless marriage with a sub-par human who is self-centered and weak."

"Magnolia." Paul trips on my name. "I've never heard you speak like that to me."

"There weren't very many truths between us, were there? There wasn't room for truth in our garden of lies."

He stays silent on the other end of the line, and I hope he's thinking of all of the years I was a good wife and mother, only loving and helpful, and careful with my words. "The truth hurts, but I've come to realize I can sell the past and buy a new, magnificent future. All it costs is acceptance. I accept that you were an awful husband. I accept that I didn't see the signs. Kendall accepts that you aren't a role model and that *she* will never be a respectable woman. The question remains if you can accept that," I say, my breaths speeding. It's therapeutic to get it off my chest like this, not having to see his face, which might make me weaker or influence my words.

Paul coughs. "I don't have a choice, do I?"

"There is always a choice. You know that. You make all sorts of choices."

"That's not fair."

"Life isn't fair," I say. "Tell her to mark down Kendall's RSVP, please."

"Yeah, yeah, Maggie. Yeah," he says, defeated, his

nasally tone telling me he's finished with our conversation as it's not going his way.

"Oh, and Paul?"

He grunts as his reply.

"Congratulations on your impending marriage. I'm sure it will bring you nothing but happiness for the rest. Of. Your. Life." I hang up the phone with a flourish.

"You are a motherfucking champion, Magnolia Sager," Jenny says, jumping up and down. "The girls are on their way back. Perfect timing." She flashes the phone screen, and the dot is heading down our road. That's the only relief I feel in this moment. "How good did that feel? I feel good for you!"

I don't feel strong. I feel weak because I'm just realizing if I'd done this sooner, I could have moved on, pieced my life back together, and found Aidan sooner. "He's upset."

"Are you really upset because he's upset?" Jenny fires.

I breathe out. It was just a realization. "I used to be. Not now. It's odd not apologizing and trying to make things right. I do feel…good." I hang my head, my coiled muscles relaxing now that conflict is finished. "Why didn't I tell him that sooner? I stayed quiet for so long."

"Aidan. Your soulful beefcake. It changes things when you care for someone, Magnolia, and makes you realize the differences between what you thought your marriage was and what it actually was. That's how it was for me." She swallows hard, setting her wineglass on the counter. "It doesn't matter how long it took, all that matters is you made it to the other side. All the things you should have done and said and known won't haunt you anymore."

I pick up my phone and see that the girls are back, parking their bikes beside the shed, the dot blinking right on top of our house. Peering out the window, I see them chattering away, talking animatedly. "My only hope is one day she's not haunted," I admit, my voice low.

"She's happy. Look," Jenny says, striding to stand next to me. "All it will take is time. More time. Kendall has made this much progress already. Let yourself be happy. Let it happen." Jenny knows. She lives inside that same place I do. That balance of being a mother and a father, fulfilling your child's needs before your own, and what that means for the guilt that comes in the nanoseconds where you do indeed think of yourself. The heart pulls in opposite directions.

"She does look happy, doesn't she?" I say, wistful.

The girls barge in through the mudroom a few seconds later, giggling wildly. "That was so much fun! A raccoon almost made me fall off my bike," Juliet exclaims, taming her ponytail. "It ran right out in front of me."

"As long as a raccoon was the only thing trying to harm you, I'm okay with that. You still have the pepper spray on that keychain in your basket, right?" I ask as visions of raccoons with red eyes and foaming mouths attacking the thing I love most in this world go floating through my head. "We might need to throw it away and get a new one. Those things might expire."

"I'm fine, Mom," Kendall says, rolling her eyes. "The pepper spray is still viable, I'm sure."

Jenny picks up her wine and takes a slow sip. "Who all was there?" she asks with narrowed eyes.

Kendall looks left, Juliet pulls out her hair and ties it up again, and I wonder if it's a nervous gesture. "Just a few girls. They were drinking, but we didn't," Juliet replies. "We just said hey and talked for a bit and then rode home. No biggie."

Kendall nods along. "Yeah, what she said."

"Which girls? Do I need to call their mothers? Are they going to make it home okay?" I inject, trying not to let my mind wander to the dark place.

"They left when we did, Mom. They're fine. Drinking a little and getting blitzed like the In Ring are two totally different things," Kendall says. She's told me about the In Ring—the cool kids who have claimed Bronze Bay as their own personal palace. They have parents and grandparents who grew up here. Their Bronze Bay roots are deep, allowing them to rule the high school and get away with almost anything. This is the first she's mentioned them drinking like college kids, though.

"The In Ring drinks a ton?" I ask.

Juliet opens the fridge and pulls out a soda.

"Of course. I don't think they own livers," Kendall says, following her friend's lead to grab a drink. They go to leave, but I have more questions.

"You'll tell me when there's drinking, right?"

Kendall flips her hair and straightens her tank top strap. "Of course. I'll always tell you if there's drinking."

Juliet and Kendall leave the room after that, and I sigh, grateful to have them under my roof, safe, locked away for at least one night. Jenny and I polish off the bottle of wine and retreat to our rooms upstairs. I hear Kendall and Juliet talking as I pass by her door. Juliet says, "I think he really likes you."

And then Kendall's reply, "I'm meeting him again tomorrow night."

My stomach sinks and my heart pounds in excitement for her, but also in fear. This is what I want. For her to form a healthy relationship with a boy. Hopefully he's a good boy who will treat her right. I don't want her to keep secrets from me, but I understand her need to be independent. I text Aidan a quick good night and pass out in a wine-induced haze.

NINE

Aidan

I SURFACE and grab the pool wall, breathing heavily. I lost count of how many laps I did after three hundred. I never lose count. Thoughts of Magnolia crept in, and I couldn't think straight, let alone keep track of my workout. I'm beginning to wonder if this is what it feels like to be obsessed. When I eat, I think about her lips. When I go for a run, I think about her body. When I'm listening to my boss drone on and on at informational meetings, I think about her wit and charm. When I'm shooting targets, I think inappropriate thoughts.

It's all so confusing.

Don't get me wrong, I've always thought about sex. Daydreams of nondescript, naked women bending in ways that aren't humanly possible. This specific Magnolia shit, though? Never. Not even once. Not even after having a rocking night with a woman who pushed all of the right buttons. Nope, still a headless person, stored in the spank bank. I spit out a mouthful of chlorinated water. She drowns me.

Hauling myself out of the pool, I rip off my goggles and throw my hands above my head to recover quicker. The indoor pool is attached to our gym on base, and I can hear weight plates clanking through grunts and groans of exertion. It's good to mix up my workout routine every once in a while to keep all of my muscles engaged. Mercer walks from the locker room, a towel slung over one shoulder. I grin when I see he's wearing his American flag Speedo and a swimming cap that says "fuck boi." We got it as a gag gift for him last Christmas, but he likes the combo more than he'll ever admit.

"How's the water?" Mercer asks.

I release my stretch and grab my towel off the rack and start drying off my shoulders. "Cool?"

"Cool? You're a regular old Einstein, aren't ya?" Mercer laughs as he positions his goggles on his eyes. They are holograms. One eye says "blow," the other eye says "me." Those weren't a gift. He found those himself.

"I zoned out," I admit, tying the towel around my waist. "The water is water. It's always the same. They're right, you know? Some chicks change everything. Even if you try your hardest to keep everything the same." I lean against the rack and peer at my phone sitting on top of the ledge.

"Are you saying you don't want change? If you didn't want change, you'd just move the fuck on. You want it," Mercer says, sitting on the edge of the pool, dangling his legs in the water.

I brush my hands through my hair, and water flies everywhere. "I don't think I have a choice."

"Seriously? You, Aidan Mixx, the elite killer, professional panty ripper, serial dater, don't have a choice? Bullshit. All you have is choices." Mercer shakes his head. His Southern accent gets deeper when he gets fired up about something, or when he talks about his home or family.

Leif appears from the same place Mercer did, grinning widely. As if he's been summoned by implied commitment. "What are you guys doing the rest of the day?" Leif asks. It's a loose schedule, and we already had our one mandatory meeting early this morning.

"I'm gonna get wet and then go make some lucky woman wet. A day full of wetness, brothers! Is there anything better?" Mercer yells, hopping into the pool with a screech. He starts stroking, heading toward the other end of the lap pool.

Leif shakes his head, but his smile drops when his gaze meets mine. "We still need to get together to talk. Want to grab lunch?" He nods his head to the doorway behind him. "Shower, then head to the diner?"

I nod. "Yeah, that's probably a good idea." Leif is married and has a baby. If anyone is going to give me useful, practical advice, it's going to be him. "How's the family?" I ask, slapping him on the back to retreat to the shower.

He smiles wide, and a weird dreamy look changes his features when he replies. And I realize it might not be obsession that I feel for Magnolia, it might be what Leif feels for his wife. That is equal parts scary and thrilling.

After lunch with Leif and all of the truth bombs he dropped, I decided to go see Magnolia. It's early afternoon, so Kendall is still in school, and Magnolia mentioned last night she was going to work at Magnolia's Steals in the morning and then work on some pieces in her garage at home. I picked up iced coffee, and I'm approaching the garage when she comes flying out, her ponytail falling out. She's wearing short shorts and a tank top. I swallow hard. The need for her is greater than anything else. I'm still getting used to it.

Magnolia spins on her heel and faces me. "Aidan!" she exclaims. Magnolia is excited, her eyes flaring when she looks at me from the top of my head down to my feet. "What are you doing here?"

I extend her drink. She takes it. "I was just leaving. A last-minute auction popped up. It's the next town over." Magnolia checks the small, delicate watch on her wrist. "I'll be home before Kendall gets home from school. Do you want to go with?" Her smile is hopeful.

"There's nothing I'd rather do than spend time with you."

She blushes and takes a sip. "They aren't selling people. Still interested?"

"I have an antique bed, remember? I'm like a secret antique collector. Do I get to sit next to you?"

"Yes. Of course. And hold a paddle if you want to."

I grin, stepping toward her. "I get to hold a paddle?"

"Yeah," she replies, nuzzling her face into my chest.

I hate that she can feel my heartbeat and knows that I'm so affected by her. Then again, it's easier this way. If my actions say one thing, perhaps my heart will tell the truth, and she'll be able to discern the difference. "You like to be spanked," I ask, leaning away to peer at her face. "Such a naughty girl." I grin.

"No one said anything about spanking," Magnolia croons, gaze darting away from mine. It's there, that fire that tells me it's not off the table. My dick hardens. "I didn't know how to work dating apps before you. Do you really think I have any experience in BDSM, Aidan?" I don't either, but fuck, would I love to do it with her in whatever capacity would satisfy her.

As we walk to her truck, I make a joke about paddling her in the middle of the auction. She blushes again and cranks her truck. Magnolia tells me it's a quick drive and makes small talk about what she's been working on and what she hopes to find today. I encourage her to keep talking. I love finding out things about her through her passion. She tells me a lot of auctions are held online these days, but she loves the thrill of the in-person ones. Nothing blows her skirt up like a bidding war. I take a mental note.

"Favorite antique?" I ask.

She scoffs, her pretty pink lips forming a pout. "There's no way I could ever pick just one," she says. She lists several things I'm unfamiliar with.

"Lie," I say. "There has to be one thing you love the most."

Magnolia stays silent in thought. "I'll need more time for that one," she finally replies. "Too hard." When she stops at a red light, she turns to look at me. "All these questions for me. Can I ask you some?"

"That's generally how a conversation works," I tease, even as my whole body tenses. This is where I lack experience. Leif said I need to be open to

Magnolia if I want to build a solid foundation for a relationship to thrive.

She clears her throat. "I want to know about your family. Not the SEALs that you call brothers. Your parents. Why don't you talk to them? Is it really that bad?"

"Cutthroat," I say, coughing a bit. How do I explain this best? Giving her something without giving her too much. Magnolia rubs one hand over her tan thigh, a nervous gesture. One that makes me hard. I shift myself as discreetly as I can. "Official couples talk about this stuff, huh?"

She shrugs. "We can do whatever we want, I guess. Whatever official means to us. I want to know because you turned out to be pretty great." She runs her hands over the steering wheel. "I'm not a prying person, you know? Not like a lot of the people in Bronze Bay, I care about you, Aidan, and I'm trying to know more about you."

Leif's words ricochet in my mind. Honesty. I have to be honest. She's not prying. I'm confident I have Magnolia pinpointed—I know her weaknesses, flaws, highlights, and quirks, even though we have only been dating for a little while. "I confess, I'm a bit of a mystery," I say. Magnolia nods and drums her fingers on the wheel to the low beat of a country song, patiently waiting for whatever I'll give her. "My parents aren't good people," I say, my heart racing as I think about the last time I saw them. The day I turned eighteen. My breathing speeds up. "You could say I'm one of those people who rise from the situation they were born into. The reason for my drive is because they were not nice folks. My mom wasn't very hands-on, and unfortunately, my father was very hands-on."

I find myself rubbing my arm, the one my father broke when I came home late one night in high school.

Magnolia looks thoughtful. "I assumed right then," she says. "That's why you never settled down. Are you afraid of having a family? Don't think I'm insinuating anything with me, we're just speaking in generalities here. You're opposed to it because of how bad your childhood was?" She swallows, and I can tell she feels bad for me. Rather, the child version of me. I don't want her sympathy. That's one thing I've never wanted. I didn't want anyone to view me as any different than my peers who came from fully functional home lives. An advantage isn't needed. Work is. I've proven myself a man.

Clearing my throat, I look out the window. "The opposite. I know I'll do it better than they ever could have imagined. I had a prime example of how not to be, how to act. I'm not afraid of settling down. That's an unfair label placed on all men who date around a lot. Can't it ever be that we haven't met the right woman?"

She stiffens, her shoulders ramrod straight.

"Of course," Magnolia says, voice quiet. "I've never thought about it that way."

Reaching over, I grab the hand working over her thigh. "Women say it all the time. Oh, I haven't met the right man. A bit of a double standard to say I date around a lot because I'm afraid of commitment, isn't it?"

Her throat works as she swallows. "It's just that you look like that, and you can have anyone you want. I can't imagine having that kind of power. I can't say I wouldn't date around just because I can if I looked as attractive as you or if my circumstances were different."

"Power? That's what you think my looks are?"

"What is it if not power?"

I squeeze her hand. "You have more power in your pinky finger than I have in my whole body then. You have no idea how appealing you are. Not just to me, but to every man in a thousand-mile radius. That's what makes you so hot."

Scoffing, she fires back, "I have a teenage daughter and a divorce under my belt. That's not appealing, Aidan, but thank you for the compliment, I think."

When she pulls into a parking spot, I pull her over to my side so I can have her nearer, smell that scent that is only Magnolia Sager. She tucks wayward strands of hair behind her ear. I kiss her head. "It was a compliment. There were multiple compliments tucked in there. One about you being hot. One about you being so awesome I want to keep you."

Saying the words out loud feels right. Honest.

She stays silent, but she does lean her head into my chest. "I'm sorry you have awful parents."

"Don't apologize, you didn't make them beat me half to death."

She winces.

I've said too much. The line was crossed.

"I can't imagine."

"You don't have to. Don't think about it. Let's go paddle each other."

"I need to ask you something," Magnolia says. "Things seem to be going well between us, right?"

"I'd like more sex, but yes, they are going well. Why do you ask?"

She sighs. "Kendall. I'm debating whether or not

to introduce her to you. Do we wait a while to make sure it's going to work out? Will she be upset I didn't introduce you two sooner?"

The kid. It's easy to forget she has a kid because she had her at such a young age. Other than the casual mentions of her daughter, I don't think about it at all. It never bothered me, but I can see how this is a big decision for Magnolia. Honestly, it's one she needs to make on her own.

"I don't know Kendall, so I'm going to say I think you need to figure that out on your own. I'm happy to meet her when you're ready…when you think she's ready. From what you've told me, she's been through a lot and I wouldn't want to add to her stress."

"Yeah," Magnolia replies, lost in thought. "You don't mind either way?"

"You'll make the right decision," I say, pulling her in tighter. "I'll sneak around for as long as you want, Magnolia. There's no pressure. I'll never put ultimatums on you like that. If you think I'll be offended, I won't. The relationship stuff is so new to me that learning the ropes and keeping this just to ourselves for a while is appealing. Meeting your daughter and getting to see the person you raised is appealing too. Don't sweat it. Make sure it's on your terms. No surprises." Like having her walk in on us fucking like animals with paddles.

"Thanks, Aidan. For being so understanding. Also, you have really great advice. Give yourself more credit with the relationship stuff," she says. Looking up to meet my gaze. "I want to kiss you right now, but I also want to go inside. If we kiss, I'm not sure the second will get accomplished."

Grinning, I lean over and whisper, "I'm good with advice and self-control. If it's a kiss you want."

Her eyes narrow. "It's not your self-control I'm worried about."

Shaking my head, I lean in and press my mouth against hers. It's a soft kiss—just enough to taste her. I pull away before I lose myself and have to invoke my control. Magnolia melts in my arms, and if I were alone, I'd bang on my chest—knowing I have her so fully. Leaning my forehead against hers, I watch her breathe. "Shall we go inside?"

"Yeah, though we might not stay long."

"No? You have things you need to get," I reply.

"Something else I need to have will take precedence," she says, sliding her hand onto the bulge in my shorts. She squeezes softly, then continues, "There are only so many hours in the day, you know?"

I run one hand through my hair, a cheek-splitting grin wrecking my face. "Magnolia Sager, I do believe you've made me blush."

"But do you agree with my plan?"

I'm losing my mind. I'm losing everything in favor of one thing. Feeding this hunger I've never felt before. She wants to know if I agree with her plan? Her chin in my hand, I kiss her more aggressively, dragging her hand back to my dick so she can feel just how much I agree. Her smile breaks our kiss. "Yes. Agreed," I say. "In case you had any doubts or wanted verbal confirmation."

She still lingers on my lips when we enter the warm garage serving as the auction house. Fans are blowing in every direction. There is air conditioning, but with all of the doors open to bring in the larger items for the auction, the heat seeps in. Magnolia looks out of place in a room full of old people. I watch her walk the perimeter searching for whatever items she's seeking. Her long brown ponytail is high, brushing her shoulders as she leans over to get a closer look at a tagged item. She looks up to where I'm standing and waves me over.

"Look at this," she says, pointing at a box of jewelry that looks like the nineties puked out. Sifting through it, she adds, "I probably need this along with that dining set." Magnolia motions to the corner where an old-ass table with six chairs sits.

I nod. "They are real gems," I exclaim, raising one brow.

She hits me on the shoulder, watching her hand as our bodies touch. "Don't pretend to know what you're talking about. Just ask me questions."

I do ask. I know everything I can possibly know about Victorian furniture twenty minutes later. We take our seats in the brown folding chairs as the auctioneer speaks faster than I knew possible. I watch his mouth as he runs through the gamut of random bobs and bits until he gets to Magnolia's dining set.

She throws her paddle up in the air and calls out a price before he can even introduce one. Another man double our age does too. And so it goes for a couple of minutes that feel like hours. I break out in a cold sweat when I realize she might not win the table, and in this moment, my heart's truest desire is that she wins. A fucking table. It's my competitive nature. I'd take out the old geezer if this were a different kind of fight. Magnolia stands up, paddle in the air, and calls out an offer significantly higher than the last one he gave. The old man shakes his head and puts his paddle down in defeat.

"Sold, number one one niner," the auctioneer calls when the bidding war concludes. I'm surprised I'm at the edge of my seat.

Leaning over, I realize she's breathing heavily. "That was intense," I remark.

"It always is," she replies, smiling at me. "I knew you'd like it."

"This table must really be worth something." I narrow my eyes at the piece of furniture once more.

"I have to fix it up a bit, but it will so be worth it." Her eyes light up.

I load the heavy set into the bed of her truck, and we're back at her house in record time. I unload the table into her workshop garage as carefully as I can, and then we're standing in the heat of her workspace, staring at each other. A drop of sweat rolls between her breasts, and I press my lips together. It reminds me of the last time we had sex. Hot sex. Sex that changed everything for me. It was sex so desperate and passionate that I can't even view her sweat without getting turned on. "Going to give me a tour?" I ask, watching her mouth, gesturing to her house with a head movement.

She nods. "We have forty minutes before Kendall gets out of school. Let's go."

There is no actual tour. She locks the door of her bedroom the second we enter, retreats to the restroom for a brief moment and then moves toward me like a lioness. I don't have time to speak a word. She's on me.

TEN
Magnolia

I KISS him like my body doesn't need oxygen. He kisses me like he might never taste me again. I thought it would be less desperate this time, but I feel the same wild connection as the first. Any time his fingers brush my bare skin, I react. His tongue is in my mouth, his hands are pinning mine above my head, and I've lost all thoughts except those of him. And us. Together.

The auction was nearly unbearable as the thoughts of what is happening right now were warping my senses. In every look, in every word spoken, Aidan conveyed how much he wanted me. As I explained patina finishes, he stared at my mouth like it was drawn by the hand of God. Or like maybe a Lladro figurine might pop out of my body. I doubt he remembers anything I said.

As his hand raises my shirt, his tongue slides up my collarbone and neck. I help pull the shirt over my head, and the cool air tickles my skin. "I've wanted to do this all day," Aidan rasps, unbuttoning my shorts and sliding them, along with my panties, down my legs. He smells like soap and his deodorant—some fresh scent that makes me think dirty thoughts. "Since the last time I had you naked," he amends when I don't respond, lost in my appraisal. "You have no idea what you're doing to me, Magnolia."

"I know what I want to be doing to *you*," I reply, grinning when I catch his gaze with mine. My stomach flips, and I hold my breath.

Aidan leans away, biting his bottom lip, in that desperately handsome way that makes me even wetter than I was seconds before. A monstrous feat, if we're being honest. "Show me," he says, muscles flexing as he raises himself off my body. "Show me what you want to do to me. Do we need the paddle?"

I shake my head. "Lie down on the bed," I say. I make the rolling motion with my pointer finger. He flips over and removes the rest of his clothing. "If you think this is weird, tell me, but I've wanted to try this since our first date." He didn't let me do anything that night. My core clenches at the vivid memory.

He smiles and takes my face in his hands. "Nothing you can possibly do to me naked will I construe as anything except awesome. Promise. Let your freak flag fly."

My heart is pounding out of my chest, and I hear my pulse in my ears. This isn't a person I've ever been. Not with Paul. Not even with myself. This is the person I'm becoming. I feel strong and out of my element. As delicately as I can, I straddle his face backward, leaning forward to slide his dick into my mouth.

Aidan's hands clasp tightly on my thighs. He pulls me down onto his face with a growl, and his lips and tongue are working my clit. It takes work to focus on my own task with his zeal for his job, the warmth from his tongue diving into my most sensitive places. I glide my hand up and down his shaft as I try to be careful with my teeth. No one ever tells you how hard it is to have something in your mouth without letting your teeth meet said object. Just another impossible standard women are supposed to live up to.

Aidan pauses his assault to readjust his grip, lifting me and lowering me at a different angle. "I could eat this pussy all day," he says, lapping at me languidly.

My breath catches, and I pick up my pace, moving my tongue against the side of his shaft. Whatever he says next is muffled by my body and his ferocious head movements. I come apart, shaking, moments later. His lips relax, his tongue licks slower, his grip loosens. I can't help but stop sucking him, my body won't allow it during the post-orgasm haze. "How are you so good at that?" I sigh, letting the haze of lust eat me alive.

"Eating is my favorite sport." I can hear the smile in his voice. "I live for cheat day, and you're the best treat."

"I need to finish for you," I sigh, catching my breath. Aidan slides a finger inside me. "I didn't anticipate being this distracted. It's your fault." Closing my eyes, I'm a slave to the pleasure he's giving me. A moan slips.

His chuckle slides over my body like a sedative. Or maybe it's because he's stroking my G-spot, but my whole body fires at his touch. I rock back onto his finger. "Want another one?" Aidan says, his tone low and gravelly. He takes my movement as my response and inserts another.

"This isn't me finishing," I moan, halfheartedly bobbing on his dick.

"This view is finishing me, Magnolia. Looking at

you, having you like this. Resisting every urge to put my cock where my fingers are."

"Fuck me, then." It's agonizing, but I slide forward, causing his fingers to leave my body, and turn to face him, my hands on either side of his hips. His face is flushed, and his lips are parted. That half-mast gaze tells me how much restraint he's using, and it's enough to make my core clench. "If you want to, that is," I add.

He flashes a grin and coaxes me up his rippled body. I detour around his clutching arms to fish out a condom from the pack in my nightstand I bought for an occasion such as this. I hold it up, victorious. "For you," I say, handing it to him. "First time shopping for them, but I got the kind I saw you had." I beam proudly at my accomplishment.

"You put it on," he says, glancing at his watch as he speaks. "Wait. We only have fifteen minutes, never mind, I rescind my offer." He snatches it, tears it open with his teeth, and has his throbbing dick sheathed in mere seconds. I'm still standing next to the bed, wide-eyed, shocked at the speed in which he completed the job. "Get over here. I want you."

His order makes my legs quake.

I glide, because I do feel like I'm floating in this moment, suspended in a place of pure elation, and join him on the bed.

Ensconced in his strong arms, he lays me beneath him. "I can still taste you on my lips. Give me more," he speaks against my lips. Aidan's kiss is furious, and it takes a second for me to catch up, to get on the same level. The palm of his hand skims down, grazing my breasts and waist until it lands between my legs. When his fingers meet wetness, he drops his head against my forehead and replaces his hand with his cock.

Aidan rocks into me in one solid thrust, and we both sigh in the sweet relief of connection. Me filled, him surrounded by me. I raise my hips to meet him thrust for thrust as he picks up his pace. We breathe together, his lips against the pulse at my throat. I can taste him, smell his skin, and I'm filled by him all at the same time. Aidan's muscles are coiled tight as he thrusts. He swallows hard as the pace of his breathing quickens, the scratch of his moans is a desperate plea for more.

Wrapping my legs around his waist allows me to rub against his pelvis at the perfect angle. "This," I say, panting, "feels so good."

Aidan grinds into me. "Not stopping until good turns into earth-shattering," he says, licking a line from my neck up to my earlobe.

My skin prickles at his touch, and my stomach dances. It's not implausible I'm having sex with Aidan right now. It's shocking how much I'm enjoying it.

He clears his throat after he lets out a huff of air. "You're so tight. I want to come right now. Magnolia, you're so fucking perfect." He kisses me on the side of the head and then presses his lips against mine, in time with his thrusts. A dance.

He could have said a million different things, and he said the one that would turn *good* into *earth-shattering*. My legs tighten as the orgasm hits. Aidan keeps his pace and comes seconds after my sexual war cry drowns into mere panting. He tucks his face into my neck. It makes me feel a way—something I'm unable to describe. Instead of my heart slowing into a normal rhythm, it batters against my chest, against him. His cock throbs one last time, deep inside me, and a bit more of his body weight presses me into the mattress.

The cool of the air skims the places where Aidan's skin isn't on mine. I tilt my head to the side, searching for him. He turns, and I'm met with his steely, intense gaze. "Is this the point where I tell you that was amazing?" he asks, a smile lighting his face.

"It was amazing, wasn't it?" I counter.

He pulls out of my body slowly. "You're a game changer, Magnolia Sager," Aidan declares, walking toward my bathroom, the used condom in hand. My bedside clock says I need to get the huge, naked man out of the house. STAT.

Aidan saunters back into the room, chuckling. His brown hair is tousled, and his muscles so damn perfect that the mere sight of him causes me to lose my breath and my manners. "If I'm a game changer, that makes you the game, right? I never want to stop playing you." That was almost an admission. Something I'm not sure I'm ready for.

He grins at me. The type of grin that would soak my panties if I were wearing them.

Sighing, I scoot off the bed. Standing in the middle of my bedroom, this man has more confidence and presence than any other man on the planet.

"We can arrange for free gameplay whenever you want," Aidan says, then his smile slips.

Crossing to him, I lay my palms on his hard abs. "Deal. What's the matter?" I ask. Trying to ignore the fact that Kendall's bus will pull up any minute.

He swallows hard and looks down at me. His jaw clenches. "You're the best thing that's ever happened to me." Taking my face in his hands, his thumb on one cheek and his pointer finger gripping the other one.

His abs rise and fall quicker than before as he gazes into my eyes, leaning closer. "Still trying to figure out what to do with that," he admits, tipping my face up to meet his lips.

I break from the kiss. "Want me to tell you what to do with it?" I ask, trying to control my pulse.

Aidan bites his lip and nods slowly, just once.

"Love me back," I whisper.

His eyes flare wide, and I think for a second I've scared him—that I've said too much, that I've been too honest. After a beat or two, his shock diminishes.

He smiles, shakes his head, takes my face in his hands again, and owns me with a kiss.

Kendall is in a bouncy mood, kicking her feet back and forth as she does her homework splayed on her bed—her earbuds in, oblivious to the fact I'm watching from her doorway. There's a shadow of guilt every second that passes that I don't tell her about Aidan. It's mostly because I feel like a completely different person, and I'm hiding it from the person I care about the most.

Paul left a message on my cell phone to tell me the child support check would be a week late. He knows it's fine, he knows my finances are in line. The inheritance from my grandparents gave me enough to begin a new life and keeps us afloat in the months when sales in the antique shop are slow. I never had to touch it when I was married to Paul, and I'd like to think my grandpa would be proud to see the life I created with what he left behind.

I'm wavering between leaving her alone and

peppering her with questions about her day. She seems happy. Happier than she's been in a long time. There's a bounce in her step. Is it possible she's thriving off of the good energy I'm putting into the atmosphere? Maybe she knows without details I'm happier? I sit next to her on the bed and lay a hand on her calf swinging in the air.

Kendall takes the earbud out of one ear and smiles. "Hey, Mom. What's up?"

"You seem happy today," I exclaim, letting my gaze take in her beautiful face. "Can I bring up a snack?"

"Nah, that's okay. I grabbed an apple when I got home. Everything okay?" she asks.

God, she can tell something is different. I panic. "No. No. I'm fine, honey. I wanted to tell you hello. Craving anything for dinner?" I lead the conversation away from happiness and back to something safe—typical.

"Something quick? I'm riding down to the beach after homework. If that's okay," she says, taking the other bud out of her ear. "Juliet will come with me." She's really trying to sell it. "And you can track me like an FBI agent using the app or whatever."

"What's down at the beach again tonight? You seeing someone? A boy?" I try to keep my tone teasing because hell hath no fury like an offended teen.

"Maybe," she replies, pressing her lips together.

"Who is it?" I ask, mentally ticking through the boys I've met that I've seen around more than a couple of times.

She smirks. "That would be bad juju. It's nothing right now, nothing special anyway. Boys seem like so much work. We're just talking. Promise. Nothing serious."

Of course I trust her, but there's a niggling feeling of something not quite right. "Sure, of course. When you're ready to talk about him."

"So, I can go?" Kendall asks, eyebrows raised.

"Sure, sure." I can't help myself, it's physically impossible. I give her the safe sex lecture and the "no means no" lecture, and when she's absolutely mad and annoyed, I leave her to finish her homework, praying my words trickle in. She's a smart girl. My hope is that she's smarter than I was.

I stop into my small bump-out office and attend to business on my laptop and head into the kitchen. My cell phone chimes with a text from Aidan.

> Jumping out of airplanes tonight. How does it feel knowing you'd be my last thought if my parachute doesn't open?

I smile.

> Morbid? And a little flattered.

> Just a LITTLE flattered?

> Fine, a lot flattered. Make sure your parachute is in full working order, though. I want free gameplay time again tomorrow.

His text response is quick.

> There's nothing else I'd rather do.

I'm smiling, the phone pressed to my chest, when Kendall walks in and asks what I'm giggling about.

I lie.

ELEVEN

Aidan

It's been about three weeks since I fell in love with Magnolia Sager standing naked in her bedroom, my heart on display in a way it's never been before. The real kind of love that drives you absolutely wild with wonderment and complete abandon.

Her daughter is at an overnight cheerleading camp for the weekend, and Magnolia showed up to my house with a weekender three hours ago. For any other man in love, this would be the best thing that could possibly happen. I'm not any other man. I want so badly for Magnolia to think I'm perfect for her. That nothing that I've done or have endured will be impressed upon what she means to me now.

She's grabbing a glass of water from the kitchen tap, humming a song that's been playing non-stop on the radio. Standing in front of the full-length mirror in my room, I give myself a mental pep talk. *You can do this. This isn't a big deal. A woman spending the night is common. Normal. I can be normal for her. For me. I deserve that. I must.*

"Do you want anything?" Magnolia calls out.

A lobotomy, a rewind button, and a dose of fuck-it-all probably isn't what she means.

"No thank you," I reply, wiping away a layer of sweat from my forehead. My friends were over at my place shooting the shit earlier. Since they left, I've received approximately ten thousand texts asking if I'm really having a sleepover or some variation of taunting-laced encouragement. The last text I read before silencing my phone was one from Mercer that said, *You've lost your goddamned mind. I better be the best man.* I didn't even reply to dispute it. Tahoe's text said, *Breathe.*

That's the one I'm currently focusing on. *In through my nose and out through my mouth.* A simple thing. Breathing. You don't even realize you're doing it most times. When you focus on it, it's the only thing you can think of. It keeps you alive.

Magnolia brushes past me to enter the bathroom connected to my bedroom. She sets her water glass down and takes her toothbrush out to begin brushing. She turns around, leaning against the counter, and looks at me while she foams her teeth, gaze narrowed and brow pinched.

I appraise her, and a little bit of nervous energy erases. She's wearing the silk pajama set I bought for her. The blue fabric brings out the color of her eyes, and the scant material barely covers anything. "You're so beautiful," I say, thinking out loud. More than I deserve. More than I can keep. My stomach knots.

She tries to respond, but toothpaste foams out of her mouth and drips down her chin. She catches it right before it gets on her top. Giggling, she finishes brushing and washing and then leans against the doorframe. "You shouldn't compliment a lady when she can't reply."

I shrug. "Had to say it the second I thought it. Your stomach looks amazing," I say, raking my gaze over her body—exposed, sun-kissed skin. "And your long legs. And your arms. Your neck." My mind wanders away from the place where I dare not go, the place that has made it impossible to sleep with anyone up until this point.

"Thank you. You're looking exquisite yourself. You're going to show me your workout early tomorrow morning, right?" I can tell she knows something is happening inside my skull, and she's trying to detour around it.

I grin. "Yeah. We'll start with a run on the beach and then we'll sneak into the gym. I'll spot you on the bench."

She shakes her head. "I have no idea what I'm doing, Aidan. I'll need more than a spot."

"You can sit on my lap. I'll give you a step-by-step gym routine."

Magnolia sways her hips, walking toward me, the silk hugging her chest, revealing peaked nipples. "I like that idea," she says, running her finger in the center of my eyebrows. "Why the frown when we're talking about gym sex?"

Running a hand through my hair, I give her the truth. "This is the part where I fuck you, Magnolia. Because it's how I forget who I am. Where I'm at and what happens next. I go to sleep alone, but…" I say, blowing out a pent-up breath.

"But what?" she asks, trailing the same finger down to my mouth, drawing her finger across my bottom lip.

I kiss her fingertip softly. She smiles. "But I don't want to do that right now. With you."

"Why?" she asks. There's no disappointment in her tone or on her face. She is genuinely curious. "You can talk to me, Aidan. Don't be afraid."

Slamming my eyes closed, I swallow down the fear. "It's how I avoid talking. Fucking, that is. Why I haven't had a real relationship. Why I'm so good at my job. It takes me away on deployments and gives me focus on things I know how to handle. It's impossible to sort what's going on in my mind."

With her delicate hands perched on my forearms, she levels me with her blue gaze. "I have an idea."

Sighing, I lean my forehead down on her shoulder. "The last time you had an idea, you sat on my face, and that led to my dick buried inside you, Magnolia."

She laughs, taking my face into her hands. "It's PG. Well, I take it back, it's triple X, but I think it will help you." Her hand slips into mine as she tugs me to follow. "You have this gorgeous claw-foot tub, and we're going to take a bath together. You're going to tell me why you don't have sleepovers, and I can give you any sordid detail you request about my past and the horrible things that plague me."

It sounds like an awful idea. Being confined in a small space without room for escape, but I track her lead and even point out a bottle of soap when she asks for something to make bubbles with. There is a solid four seconds after she takes off her shorts and shimmies the top over her head that I think of nothing except my dick and her pussy dancing the mamba, but then she commands me to get in the water. I do. And I'm not thinking, I'm just going along with what she requests, and that makes it easier. Not having to make decisions or think about scenarios. I exist with her, and it's so refreshing I could cry.

I lean against one side of the bathtub, and her back props against the other, our legs are entangled. The warm water eases my muscles, and I relax.

Her foot brushes my hard-on, and I catch it with both hands, massaging my thumb into the pad of her foot. "I hate to say this was a good idea, but you're right. This was a good idea," I say.

"I have good ideas every once in a while. Been around for a while, you know? Gotta be right every now and then. It's just odds." She winks, and her eyes turn heavy as I deepen the massage, taking one foot in both of my hands. Magnolia sighs and leans her head back completely. "I'm going to rest my eyes. Get it off your chest, Aidan. Tell me everything. If you want me to be quiet, I can do that. If you want me to participate in conversation, I can do that, too. I'm a good listener."

I expect a knee-jerk reaction to rise. My heart rate to rocket or my stomach to lurch, but it doesn't. No urge is known, except my desire to tell her my truths. There are several different places I could start or things I could say that would explain quite easily how messed up I am. I decide to start at the beginning instead. It's a place no one else has had access to.

"My name means 'fire' in Gaelic," I say, clearing my throat. Magnolia's eyes pop open. "Once, when my father was beating me, he said he wouldn't stop until he snuffed me out completely. I thought he'd succeed. Back then, you know? When I was a kid and I had no clue how the world worked, when you only know what your parents tell you? I thought one day he would kill me. Extinguish me completely." Magnolia is staring at me now, hard, not even trying to possess the ability to play it cool. I grin. "It's okay. I think I turned out pretty normal," I say. "All things considered."

She shakes her head, beautiful eyes turning down in the corners. Clearing my throat, I go on. "He was beating me that time because he found me brawling with a teenager who lived at the end of our street. That kid was a real prick who bowed up if you looked at the grass by his sneaker wrong. I was riding my bike, and he threw a rock at me. Typical boy stuff I realize now, but back then my father made it seem like I'd committed a mortal sin." The memory isn't as strong as it once was. I'm letting it slip, after all this time. Finally. "It was confusing, you know? He wanted me to be a man, and that's what he always preached, but then something as testosterone-fueled as fighting was off-limits. I never knew what he wanted from me. Only that he seemed to hate me and everything about my personality. I never lived up to what he wanted."

"So he beat you…a lot?" Magnolia whispers. "If questions aren't okay, tell me." She presses her pink lips together.

I shake off her question. "When I was eighteen, I also learned that St. Aidan was an Irish saint. Not that it was the only reason I changed my mindset, but it gave me some perspective. Things could seem one way and in actuality be quite the opposite. I understood that what my parents put me through didn't have to define me, not on a surface level."

Magnolia clutches my calves in a death grip like I might disappear. Her mouth is open, and I fear she might ask something else.

"I became a SEAL. The manliest career path I could find. I could make a difference in the world, too.

Thank God I hacked it and made it through training. I was really fucked up back then. I had single-minded focus and something to prove, except I resented my reasons for choosing this job. I grew to love it eventually, and now I know there's nothing else in the world that would make me happier."

"Your mom didn't stop it?" Magnolia asks, wincing. "She's your mother." Her lips praise the last word. As they should.

I try to smile, but it reflects as a grimace. "All mothers aren't as wonderful as you are. That's a sad fact. Looking back, I think she honestly thought he was doing what was best for me. Turning me into a man." I swallow hard, remembering all the times I went to my mother hoping for her warm arms of comfort and got turned away instead. "I have to believe she was misguided and feared him as well. The alternative is she had a child she didn't love. That's sadistic by anyone's standards, right?"

A tear falls down her face as she shakes her head. "I can't fathom someone not loving you."

"Because you're a good person," I choke out.

"No, because you are so wonderful, smart, kind, selfless, perfect, and lovable. You are caring, Aidan. You would lay down your life to protect our country, for strangers you've never met. You are a *saint*."

I squeeze her foot. "I'm a little bit fire, too, though, right?" My voice breaks.

"Only in the bedroom," she agrees, choking on an exasperated sob.

"Deal," I say. I sigh out a long breath and turn my face to the bubbles—away from her piercing gaze. "My father beat me when I slept in my bed. He told me real men sleep on floors. It hardens us, makes us strong instead of feeble. It's irrational. Completely and utterly irrational. He slept in a bed. I never thought anything of it back then. I just assumed that he'd learned his lessons like I was doing, and now he got to have comfort. He'd proved himself already. How fucked up is that?"

"You had a bed in your room but weren't allowed to sleep in it?"

I nod. "I have a hard time sleeping because of the years I spent on the floor or sleeping with one eye open when I was *supposed* to be on the floor. I hate that it's affected me, but it's the one thing that lingers. The very last fucking remnant of Cosby Mixx that is left in my body. I'm sorry, Magnolia."

"Why are you apologizing to me?" She leans up and straddles my legs. "Look at you," she whispers, laying a bubbly hand on the side of my face. "Look at how magnificent you are despite the role model you had." She shakes her head and pecks my lips gently. Leaning away, I realize her eyes are glassy. "Who cares if you have to sleep on the floor? Or a counter? Or a bed? Or on a cliff in Timbuktu? I don't care, that's for sure. Aidan, I'm here, hand on your heart, because I love you and all that encompasses. Never be ashamed of your past. It doesn't determine your future. You do." Her hand slides down the side of my neck and ends on top of the right side of my chest.

My throat clogs, and I have to close my eyes against the onslaught of emotions brought forth. I pull her warm body against mine as close as I can get her, and she tucks her face into my neck. "You do," I say, inhaling the mix of soap and skin.

She stiffens in my arms. "I do what?"

"You determine my future, Magnolia."

Her neck works as she swallows. I speak before she can respond. "I've never told a woman about my past. Never thought I would, either. Not because I'm ashamed. Why would someone else care? What am I achieving by being honest? Nothing." The magnitude of what I've just done hits me square in the chest, and a pang of anger tinged with relief washes over me. "It's you. It's all you," I say, slamming my eyes closed.

"Why did you tell me?" Magnolia asks, breaths pushing against my skin, in cool contrast to the water surrounding us.

"I want you to know me," I reply. "And having your hand on my heart feels right. The only thing that's felt this right in my entire life."

Magnolia clutches my pec muscle tighter, and her breasts graze my body as she breathes in deeply, steadying her voice. She whispers praise—affirmations, things I'd be embarrassed about if anyone else heard, but things I crave to hear nonetheless, sentiments that mean more than she realizes because they are words that have never been spoken before. Not to me. I shake my head in disgust—for the fact I've waited my entire life for this kind of validation.

Her voice is low and steady, punctuated with a fierce, loyal love I've never known from a woman, just from the SEAL brotherhood. Magnolia lists the things she loves about me and takes the pieces of the little boy hiding under the table and puts him back together. Maybe not perfectly, but there's a sense of wholeness when she holds me and speaks like this. Shuddering, I let my whole body relax completely—all the tension of holding this in for my entire life. Magnolia puts her hands on either side of my face. "Do you want to see your parents again?"

I shake my head. "I can't." I don't want to. Saying 'can't' seems easier. There's a finality in the word can't. There's a reason parents always tell their children not to say it.

Licking her lips, she casts her gaze sideways. "You can, Aidan. It might be what gives you closure, letting you move on completely. I'll go with you if you want. Don't you want him to know you aren't broken?"

I've considered this for many years, thinking about what it might be like to face them both again. Over the years, they've tried to reach out to me, but after a bit of dodging them, they gave up. In a twisted way, I think my father will take credit for how I've turned out. That he alone is responsible for my successes.

My stomach flips, and I hold my breath. "I don't want them to get an ounce of satisfaction," I say, trembling at the thought.

"You could tell him that you strived to become the opposite of him in every way. It's not like you're imagining it," Magnolia states, pressing her full lips into a firm line.

For the first time during this whole conversation, my dick responds to the naked woman sitting on my lap. She feels it and smiles. "Seriously. You should think about it."

I agree. She asks where they live and what they do, and I tell her as much as I know about them, or rather what I last knew about them, and I can see the wheels spinning behind her crystal eyes. Telling her to stop formulating whatever plan she's concocting is moot. I've come to realize once she sets her mind on something, there's little that will get in her way. I like that about her. Love it, in fact.

There are several silent seconds in which we regard

each other with new, faultless eyes. That truthful moment when you discover a new layer of a person and love them a little more for it. She burrows deeper—seeping into the cracks between those detached pieces, repairing my soul, caulking the errors, and smoothing over the imperfections with a tender grace. Taking the side of her face into my wet hand, I bring her lips to mine. The kiss is a flutter of wet lips and breaths.

"Thank you," she says, brushing her mouth against mine. "For being honest with me. It makes me feel a little better about showing you my dumpster fire."

"Making this about you now?" I tease, nipping at her bottom lip.

She groans. "No, I mean maybe. Whatever you want."

I chuckle. "Whatever I want? That's a brave statement, Ms. Sager."

She quirks one brow. "We aren't talking about life dumpster fires anymore, are we?"

I shake my head slowly, letting a lopsided grin slip.

"Oh, my," Magnolia says, eyes flaring wide, neck working as she swallows hard. "Then one question remains."

Chuckling, I ask, "Just one?"

She nods once, the large topknot on her head bobbing forward. "What do you want?" Magnolia asks, her gaze locked with mine.

My heart pounds against my chest so rapidly I know she can feel the shift, knows my thoughts even if I didn't say a word. "Be more specific, Magnolia," I tease. "What do I want now? What do I want next month? Next year? What do I want in the next century?" Her eyes narrow as she contemplates how to respond, and I lose myself in the perusing the shape of her body—the parts that aren't hidden by water, the sections of skin that belong to my gaze alone. Belong to me.

She licks her lips. I watch.

"I'll answer my own questions. I want you, Magnolia. You're the answer."

Magnolia smiles with her eyes. "That's pretty flattering."

"It's truth," I counter, clearing my throat. Speaking so many truths consecutively feels odd.

"As long as you're not the problem," she says, stepping out of the bath in one languid movement. Bubbles slowly slide down her naked body—crawling down her flat stomach, dripping down toned legs, sliding between her legs as water falls off her peaked nipples.

My mouth waters as I shake my head in disbelief. How lucky am I?

Magnolia extends her hand down to help me stand up, and I take it. "I have another idea," she announces when my wet body is pressed against hers on the small bath mat in front of the tub.

"I might have to shoot it down if it's not the same as my idea."

Cool and confident, she replies, "It's the same idea."

Magnolia licks a drop of water off my chest while looking up at me through thick, black lashes.

"Thank God," I murmur, letting my eyelids fall to half-mast.

TWELVE

Magnolia

I SHOULD TELL him it doesn't matter. That we can get over everything from our pasts together, but that's a cliché, and it's probably a lie. No one ever truly gets over anything traumatic. We shove it down into the corners of our psyche and pray it doesn't bubble up during inopportune times. Like when you want to have a sleepover for the first time. Or when you go on a first date. I think my honesty upfront about the divorce and affair is why we're here right now. Existing in this unfamiliar territory of honesty and love stripped bare. It could just be perfect timing or destiny. Was my entire life planned before it began? If I had met Aidan Mixx earlier in my life, would anything have changed? Would I never feel this all-consuming passion with anyone if one thing threw my path off course?

I'm still quivering, coming down from the last orgasm Aidan gave me, wrapped in a sheet, on the floor in his living room. The moon is shining in through the window, making the reality look a little more romantic than it actually is. I made a huge pallet bed on the floor with all of the blankets, pillows, and comforters I could find in his linen closet and on his bed. It's not uncomfortable, it's also not a bed, but he deserves to be understood. Even if it's at the expense of my own comfort. "You can go sleep on the bed, Magnolia," Aidan whispers into the dark space between our sweaty bodies. "You don't have to stay here. In fact, I must insist you sleep comfortably."

"This was my idea, I'll remind you. I want to sleep where you are. I am perfectly comfortable right here."

He pulls me toward him and tucks me into his big spoon. I sigh, and a little more security washes over me, his bicep now tucked under my head. I close my eyes against the physical and emotional exhaustion. I'm almost asleep when Aidan says lowly against my ear, "I didn't tell you the most important thing." His tone is provocative, a luring call I can't resist.

I turn in his arms to face him.

I kiss his lips that still taste like me.

"I love you, Magnolia."

I grin at his proclamation. "You do?"

"I said it, didn't I?" he replies. He kisses me once more. "I always mean what I say."

"I was the one who told you to love me," I add.

"You can't control me, woman," Aidan growls, taking my lip between his teeth. "I love who I want."

"You've loved many women in your past?" I pull away so I can see his gaze in the dim light.

Aidan shakes his head. "Only you could turn this life-shattering moment for me into an inquisition."

"No," I counter. "I need to know so I know how seriously I should take it." Smiling, I run my hand through his messy hair.

He sighs, and it's kind of a groan. "If you flipped

through my mental dictionary, there would be a photo of you next to the word 'love.' Just a photo of you."

Grinning, I ask, "Am I naked though? In the picture next to the definition?"

"You're impossible." He controls my head, and forces me into a passionate kiss.

He leaves me gasping for air—dizzy with emotion. "I love you, Aidan."

He leans in to kiss me once more, slowly this time. I can't tell you how much time passes before we eventually fall asleep. When I wake to the morning sun blazing in the windows, his heavy arms are still wrapped around my body. I'm hyperaware of every place his skin meets mine and how his breaths seem to align with my own.

I sneak my hand out of the tangled sheet to reach my phone to check I haven't missed any calls or texts from Kendall. "Don't think about leaving me," Aidan says. "Weren't we going to work out?"

"So bossy. You know I work on the weekends," I say. "We slept in too long, and orgasms took precedence over the workout. You can come and hang at the shop with me. I have about a dozen orders I need to get ready to ship. I'd never say no to an extra pair of hands."

My statement gave him other ideas. Aidan slides his warm hand down the side of my body and wedges my legs apart to work his fingers against my clit. I moan out. "Yeah, I'd never say no to these hands," I correct, panting.

He pulls away, dragging his fingers up my stomach. "That could be fun."

It takes a lot of effort, but I roll away from him. "I have to get stuff done. For real. You can't distract me all day, and anyway, I was thinking," I say, pausing as I gaze at his huge frame barely covered by the dainty sheet. He is a walking, talking, magnificent distraction. One I'll probably always be fussed by.

Aidan folds his arms behind his head. "Thinking isn't good for you." He smirks, appraising my naked form with glee.

"If you think it's a good idea, maybe it's time for you to meet Kendall? She gets back from camp tonight. We could have dinner at the house and see what kind of awkwardness ensues. Or if you'd rather not meet her, I understand that too. It's just that I'm confident that the way I feel about you isn't going to change anytime in the foreseeable future, and if I'm gauging things right, you feel pretty ardently as well?"

"You are precisely correct, madam."

"Then you think this is the right thing to do? To introduce you to her? I've checked most of the internal boxes. I've met your friends, I know your backstory, and you live by a moral code, at least with regard to your profession. You probably have a clean background check."

"I'm even CPR certified and have a negative TB test on file," Aidan quips, his smile growing, dimples popping. "I'd be honored to meet her. We can play it cool. However you want. Depending on what you're comfortable telling her. I can be long-lost Uncle Slappy or the guy who is going to help you spruce up the house and fix the garbage disposal—I'll be whoever you want me to be. This is all you, baby." He bites his lip after he calls me "baby," unsure if he can get away with it.

I swing my hands on my hips, and his gaze follows my movement. "Or I can be the man who spends the night and makes her mom scream all night long." He rolls over to his side and props his head on his hand, waiting for my response like an excited schoolboy.

"I'm not even going to dignify that inappropriateness with a response, Mixx."

I find myself checking him out even as I take steps backward toward his bedroom, where my clothing is somewhere on the floor. He knows what he does to me. It's evident in the way he uses his muscles to sit up. An offense of abs, I'll call it. My throat clogs, and I take another step, quicker this time.

"Careful, Magnolia. You're liable to trip and fall directly on my cock. Wouldn't want that when you have so much to do today. Would we?"

I turn around then and bolt for his bedroom and close the door against his low, manly chuckling. I'm losing my mind. It's the only explanation. Even as my subconscious feeds me another, more logical reason I'm acting like a completely feral woman. Never, not once in the years I was married to Paul, did I feel this draw—this craving to be connected to a man like this. Last night Aidan bared his soul and gave me horrifying details that provided answers about his personality. And his life choices. The mothering instinct in me wants to help him reconnect with his family, but logic dictates his family doesn't deserve to glimpse his face ever again. I'd also like to keep him as my own for the rest of time. Let's not forget that selfish fact.

I tap my pointer finger on the door repeatedly. "Maybe just a quickie," I whisper to myself. "I am already wet," I reason like it's an everyday problem I'm trying to solve, instead of fighting against my own will. What would it hurt to be five minutes more? Slowly, I unlock the door and push it open, all resolve lost somewhere. Aidan is standing there, his massive naked frame propped against the wall, a sardonic grin plastered on his face. It's disconcerting how cool and collected he seems at any given time. More so now that I know what he's hiding and how much he's confided in me. It's still there, that stoic, alpha presence that makes me weak in the knees. Is that the product of hormones…or love?

"Ready to fall on my dick?" he growls.

I blow out a long, defeated breath. "We have to be fast." I look at my cell phone to check the time and then set it down on the table next to the door. "Condom?" I ask. His gaze meets mine, and I see the decision written on his expression.

Aidan stalks toward me, erection bobbing as he takes me into his burly arms. He leans down and whispers in my ear, "You okay if we don't use a condom?"

I nod, biting my lip. "Yes." It will be the first time we haven't used one, and it makes my head swim.

"Okay, well, *you* need to be fast." His hand slides between my legs. When he finds wetness, he dips down, picks me up, and thrusts his dick inside while turning so my back presses the wall. I let out a loud squeal when he slides in and out of me. Aidan lays his forehead against mine, and it only takes a few minutes before we're both slick with sweat and on the brink of orgasm—his throaty growls of pleasure pushing me closer to the brink.

Skin slaps and his hands dig into my ass as he groans against my neck. I hold my breath as the pleasure rolls inside me, my whole body tensing at the peak. Collapsing in his arms, I'm no adversary for his thrusts, but it's only a few more pumps before he jerks, cum funneling deep within my body. He always comes after me. Always.

"How do you come at the right time, every time?" I breathe, leaning off his shoulder, to brush his tousled brown hair off his face. "It's unnerving."

"You don't like it?"

I quirk a brow. "I love it. Just didn't know it was a thing. That men had control of the when."

He chuckles, and his face is devastatingly handsome. His eyes are clear, and that freaking smile is so genuine it hurts. "I've told you everything else anyway, might as well tell you the truth."

"That bad?" I pry. Aidan's gaze is locked on my mouth.

He licks his lips. "No, I just think about not coming. It takes every single cell in my body to join in the effort to not come. Sometimes I pray you come. That's why, when I told you to tell me what you like, it's actually for me." A blush crosses his cheeks. "That was the single most amazing feeling in the world, by the way. We can never use a condom again."

"Selfish, Aidan Mixx," I counter, my mouth open in mock outrage.

"But I do have *your* best interests at heart. Don't forget that." He sighs. "I don't want to let you leave. I want to stay inside you all day."

My eyes flutter closed as I concentrate on our joined bodies. I flex my core, and he jerks one more time inside of me. "I'd like that," I whisper. He trails a kiss along my dewy neck and ends at the bottom of my ear. "I'd like that very much. But…"

He cuts off the rest of my sentence with a kiss as he grinds his pelvis against my clit. It's at least thirty seconds of agonizing bliss, knowing it's the end and I have to leave the throes of our perfect night. When Aidan pulls away from the kiss, he pulls his cock out of my body and lets me slide back down to my feet, panting, gazing at him like a wild animal seeking prey. I want more of him. The need is carnal.

His eyes are narrowed, and his brow furrows as his chest rises and falls up and down. His appearance mirrors my emotions exactly. Down to breaths—his tendons and muscles contracting and flexing, gaze flicking over every inch of my body like a territorial animal.

"You have to go," he says, voice cracking as he finishes my sentence.

"I do," I say.

"Then go," Aidan says, opening his arms wide, an invitation to disobey his halfhearted order.

I steady myself by pushing off the wall. "Come with me," I reply, taking tentative steps toward his bedroom. He's still looking at me, like that, and I still desire him in every single way imaginable. "Please," I test.

He smiles, shaking his head. "As if I have an option at this point."

He picked me up from middle school every Wednesday. When I was eleven, I remember speed walking through the open-air corridor toward the front of the school, excitement coursing through my body because it was the end of the school day and because my grandpa would be waiting. He was always the first in the pickup line, leaning against the side of his burnt orange pickup truck with a cap on, his passenger-side door open—waiting for me. It was the equivalent of a red-carpet welcome, and it made my heart squeeze with love every single week. Grandpa's face would split into a beatific smile the second I rounded the corner. I never had to guess, I knew that picking me up from school was the very best part of his day. Do you know what that feels like? To be somebody's best part?

After he'd smile, he'd open his arms and say, "There's my squeaky-mo! How was your day, kiddo?" I'd hug him from the side, around his big ole belly, and he'd kiss the top of my head as I told him about my day. Grandpa said I squeaked instead of cried when I was a newborn, and he called me that nickname every day. I liked it. It was only mine.

I'd climb into the cab of his truck, and he'd close the door behind me. I'll always remember the scent. The antique polish and the dusty smell of old things. The back of his truck was always filled with antiques of every shape and size. I'd ask if he found any treasures while he was at yard sales and the flea market, and Grandpa would tell me, in detail, about every "super find" he purchased. I listened, intent on every single word, because if he derived that much happiness from his treasures I wanted to learn all I could. As he spoke, he waved at the kids as we passed them walking from school, and he smiled so big and so wide that it made me happy being in his proximity.

When I was eleven I didn't care, would never think to be embarrassed by his funny words or open affection. His bad heart made sure he didn't live long enough for that to happen, and a lot of the time I'm happy about that. What would his face look like when he picked up the angry teenage version of me and my face was pointed at the ground, cheeks red? How would he take it when he found out the best part of his day was the worst part of mine? What would he think of all the time I spent ignoring my passion? The devastation of my marriage crumbling would have killed him. The memory of what could have been chokes me as I check out an older gentleman, taking care to wrap the ceramic carefully with newspaper.

"She's going to love this," I reaffirm.

He smiles, exposing a section of gums. "Surely she will. I thank ya, Miss Magnolia. You always have the treasures I'm huntin'."

I thank him for stopping in and link my arm in his to walk him to the door. I watch his back as he hobbles down the street to the nearby florist, and I think of my grandpa some more, wistful and happy that I've finally built something out of our shared love for antiques. Finally have a life I love even if it took the whole thing falling apart first.

Aidan clears his throat from behind me. "My competition is looking a little decrepit," he says, striding from the back room where I had him packaging online orders. It was a killer week, and business is picking up as it always does this time of year.

"He was buying a gift for his wife," I deadpan. "I'm not into the elderly, although you might fit into that category. Geezer."

He presses his lips together. "Was that a burn? Did you just try to zing one on me?" He raises one brow, and my stomach flutters. "Am I bringing you to the dark side? Is it fun?"

I roll my eyes—an attempt at outward dismissal.

Everything internally loves when he acts cocky and sarcastic. "Are you finished with the orders?" I change the subject.

"I've been finished. What else do you have for me?" he asks. "Maybe something wet?"

Shaking my head, I look around and realize the store is clean, everything is ready to be shipped, and I've begun plans for the shop window display for Christmas. Aidan helped a bit, and he's already told me he wants credit for his design skills. "I think it might be time to wrap it up. I'm going to pick up Kendall from school, and you could swing by for dinner in a few hours? If you're still up for it?"

He folds his arms across his burly chest. "Up for it? When have I never been up for something?"

"Oh my gosh! Stop joking about this. This is a big thing, Aidan." Spinning away, I bolt the door and flip the sign to Closed. His hands encompass my waist before I can turn.

He leans down and whispers into my ear, "I know it's serious. I'm sorry. It's hard being this close to you when we're alone."

He smells like the back room. Like polish and dust. Like memories. Tilting my chin up, I meet his devilish gaze. "What's your best part of the day? The very best part of every day?"

Aidan pulls away but keeps me locked in his arms, his face contemplative. "It's different depending on the day," he replies.

"Tell me what you mean."

Clearing his throat, his eyes dart to the window behind my head. "In San Diego, the best part of my day was anytime I was out on the water, the shoreline in my peripheral, the ocean to the other side, the temperature is always perfect. Not too hot or too cold. It was…the best." Aidan pauses and meets my eyes. "The best part of my day when I'm deployed is when I'm not on. When I can take off the gear, strip down to my underwear, and be free. When I can wipe it all clean. That's the best part of my day. The emptiness."

I can't help myself. The energy of truth feels like a drug. I need more. More of his thoughts and feelings. "What about here? What's the best part of your day here? In Bronze Bay?"

Aidan raises one brow and nods. "Sunrise on the water. I can see it so much better here. I didn't live on the water when I lived in San Diego. I just worked at the beach. Why do you want to know?"

Biting my lip, I tip my head to the side. "I think it's important. That's all." Hesitating a few seconds, I tell him a bit about my grandpa.

He nods, eyes smiling. Aidan seems happy when I open up. I think he must feel relieved there are other pieces of me that Paul hasn't scarred and blazed to the ground. He leans down and kisses me, then dips me back even further as he deepens the kiss. I giggle against his mouth. I'm breathless and can still taste him on my tongue when I pull away.

"Can I bring anything tonight?"

"Just your bravery and common sense."

He scoffs. "As if you had to tell me that." He flexes a bicep.

I roll my eyes, but can't deny my core clenches as I admire him. I lead him to the back door and lock the door behind us, the blinding heat hitting us like a brick.

When I get to my car, I turn to say, "Hey Aidan."

He grins in reply. "This was the best part of my day."

He grins wider. The smile that makes my stomach flip. "Day's not over yet, Magnolia."

THIRTEEN
Aidan

I KNOCK the wall in Magnolia's living room with the side of my fist. "These walls seem pretty sturdy," I say, gaze flicking to Magnolia. Kendall is sitting on the sofa scrolling on her phone. Dinner was quiet, her daughter only speaking when her mother prompted her to respond.

Magnolia's neck works as she swallows. I let my grin spread wider. "They are, but it will be easy to open up the one in the upstairs hallway to get to the electrical." I'm under the guise of a repairman and a friend. Magnolia choked when introducing me to Kendall and I helpfully supplied the profession. I know this has to be hard for her. Difficult in the way that anything is when you don't have any experience with it. I'm in it for the long haul so I'm willing to take baby steps even if it makes my chest hurt not being able to touch her. "You're sure that's where the electrical is for the ceiling fan, down here?"

Magnolia nods and casts a furtive glance at her

daughter. "Kendall, can you think of anything that needs to be repaired in your bathroom?"

Kendall looks up, both eyebrows raised. "No, Mom. Is there anything you can think of that needs to be repaired?" Her sentence is laced with venom.

"Don't talk to me like that, young lady. What has gotten into you?"

Kendall drops her phone on the cushion next to her and clasps her hands on her lap. In a move that tells us, even me, a person unskilled with kids, she's going to unleash some sort of demon. "Stop lying to me, Mom. He's not a repairman," Kendall snaps. "I'm not an idiot. Don't treat me like one. Can I go to my room?"

I clear my throat and draw two sets of eyes. "I can repair anything," I deadpan. It's a semi-lie. If I can't fix it, my bros will know how. That's the same thing.

Magnolia puts up a hand to silence me.

"I wasn't sure how you would react if I told you I was dating Aidan, Kendall. Everything is tricky—tedious. I'm not lying to you," she says, shaking her head. "I love you, and I wanted to do what was right by you."

"Mom," Kendall fires. "The second he walked into the house, I knew what he was to you. I'm not some child you need to shelter. Dad messed that up, remember? You are my person. The person I trust. I'm old enough to recognize," Kendall says, pausing while she glances at me and then back to her mother, "whatever it is between two people who...like each other. It's obvious to me, so please don't treat me like a child."

I take a breath for the first time in at least thirty seconds and put one hand in my pocket. With the other hand, I hike a thumb over my shoulder. "I can let you guys talk?"

"No," Magnolia says, patting the seat next to her on the loveseat. "Sit down."

This is a lot to take in. I realize now how serious of a thing this conversation is. I break out sweating. I'm barging into this broken home, claiming a position that has been vilified up until this very second. Crossing to her, I sit. She takes my hand and squeezes hard.

"I'm sorry, Kendall. I'm sorry," Magnolia says.

"It was actually me who did the lying if we're being technical," I offer.

Kendall glares at me. "What are your intentions for my mother?"

Magnolia starts to speak, but I cut her off. "I'm going to fix the ceiling fan first and foremost," I announce. Kendall grins. Magnolia sighs. "Then I'm going to make sure nothing else breaks."

"How can you do that?" Kendall asks, raising one brow.

I've been hooked up to lie detectors at least a dozen times. There is training we're given on how to be deceitful and how to sway the test in our favor. I'm good at it. Right now, though? I'm sweating like a whore in church. Honesty is the only option.

"Well," I say, clearing my throat. "I guess I can't promise nothing else will break, but I will always be here to fix it. I might not be a perfect repairman, but I'm a quick study. I'll always give it my all. Your mom is the most amazing woman I've ever met in my life. I'd fix anything for her."

Kendall is silent, contemplating her next attack, I'm sure. I glance at Magnolia, and her eyes are glassed over.

She sniffles once and says, "Kendall, I'm happy. Aidan makes me happy in a way your father never did, but you are my first priority. If you are uncomfortable having Aidan around, just say the word and we can continue our relationship out of your world." Magnolia shakes her head. "I wouldn't be offended in the least. I'm serious. You are more important than anything else."

It's in this moment that I realize what everyone says about parenthood is true. After children are born, there is a change, and everything revolves around them. There is a small itch inside that wants me to be jealous of the fact that Magnolia will never be only mine. However, the rational fact is, Magnolia is a good mother. A mother I wish I had. A mother I'd want for my own children if that day ever arrives. That is what matters. She releases my hand and folds herself into Kendall, giving a giant hug.

"Do you think I'm some sort of monster, Mom? Of course I don't care if he's around," Kendall sniffles, burying her face in Magnolia's long dark hair. "I was just upset that you lied to me. I've known. You've been acting different. Something has been up. Keep me in the loop."

Magnolia pulls away and wipes at Kendall's tears with her thumbs and tucks her hair, the same shade as her own, behind her daughter's ears. I'm an intruder in this moment, but I can't look away, can't stop reliving a childhood when my only wish was to have someone wipe my tears.

I've never wanted something more than I want Magnolia in this moment. I want to make her mine forever. For everything she is. For everything she isn't. I'll give her everything I can give her and make sure she knows she's loved and knows that Kendall will always be cared for.

"Kendall," I say, my voice cracking. Both of them look at me, and it's a little jarring how similar they look when they're upset. My heart pounds as the adrenaline hits. "Your mom is the very best part of my life."

Their smiles are identical, and an emotion washes over me. An unfamiliar feeling. The best way to sum it up is: mine.

"Okay, okay. Enough of this. I have ice cream for dessert. Let's hear all about the camp, okay?" Magnolia blurts out.

Kendall opens up, the wedge that was there through dinner is gone. She's a happy, bubbly teenager. Truth. That's all it took. All that was required to gain her favor. Magnolia squeezes my side as she passes by on her way to the freezer. The dynamic in our world has changed, and I like it.

I'd do anything to keep it.

Anything.

"Tell me about yourself. I already know you came to town when *that base* did," Kendall says, grabbing my attention.

"I did. I love Bronze Bay. It's been good for me," I reply, meeting Magnolia's gaze. "It's been slow lately."

"You're a Navy SEAL then?" she asks, eyes big and rounded. She already knows I am, she just wants to hear me say it.

Clearing my throat, I form the speech in my head and change it to the truth. "Yes. I am."

"That's so cool. So, you can, like, kill anyone?" Her tone is hedging on sarcastic.

I grin. "Not just anyone," I say, biting my bottom lip to stifle a laugh.

"That's enough about that, Kendall," Magnolia chides, setting a bowl of ice cream in front of her daughter. "You mentioned you were riding your bike down to the beach again. Isn't it a little late? Juliet isn't here either. I'm not sure if I'm okay with you going down there by yourself. Are you meeting that boy again?"

Kendall pauses, and her gaze darts left. She's going to lie. Most definitely. "No, Mom. It's a group of people like before. No drinking or drugs or illegal activities. Plus, don't you want some alone time?"

Oh, she's good. Really good.

"No," Magnolia replies. "But I guess you can go. Tracking on your phone. We can rent that movie when you get back?" Her tone is hopeful, with that right amount of desperation that I imagine a teen needs to hear to be agreeable.

"Sure, Mom. That sounds great. Will Aidan be joining us for a movie?"

I shake my head. "No. No. I've occupied enough of your mom's time this weekend. It should be a girls' night." I'd love nothing more than to infringe on movie night, but I need to find my place, and rushing things won't bode well for my long-term goals. Patience. That's what will get me to the end zone.

Kendall shrugs. "You can stay if you want. I don't care." She pauses, seems to consider something, and turns to face me, chin tilted up. "I'm just going to say it. Word on the street is you're a bit of a player, Aidan. Not only that, but you like younger women. It's not my place to say anything," Kendall says, apologizing to her mom, and continues. "Don't be that kind of person. That's what I wanted you to know…" Magnolia looks shocked her daughter has spoken with such fierceness on her behalf. "So, yes, you can stay, but I'm on to you." Kendall looks away.

I clear my throat. "I can assure you I have the best intentions and don't have any plans to hurt your mom in any way. I do appreciate your fire," I say, grinning. Kendall's straight face stays in place. "I mean it. You received bad information from the Bronze Bay rumor mill."

Kendall nods and sighs, long and hard. I reassure her once more. "I can't stay for a movie tonight. I have stuff to do at home and an early alarm. Rain check for sure, though."

Magnolia looks disappointed, but I know I'm making the right decision. I shovel the last scoop of ice cream in my mouth, wash my bowl, and bid my farewells as effortlessly as I can make them seem. Kendall grunts and waves, and Magnolia walks me out to the mudroom. Her eyes are wide and beautiful. I blink a couple of times to erase my stymie.

"Thanks for tonight, Aidan. That could have gone awry, and you reined it back in. Sorry for Kendall. The gossip around here really is something." Magnolia shakes her head. "You're so good. I can't believe my luck. Thank you." She goes on her tiptoes and kisses me quickly on the cheek. We're far enough from the dining table that Kendall can't hear us, but she would be able to see our heads above the swinging doors that separate the kitchen and mudroom.

"Hey," I say. "I was honest. I think that's the best course of action for me. I caution you that I have no idea what I'm doing. This is all fly-by-the-seat-of-my-pants, but I'll always try. Okay? Know that."

"I know," Magnolia replies.

Kendall flies past us both, hitting the screen door at

a bolt. "Riding my bike down to the beach. I have my cell. I'll be home in an hour, Mom. Nice meeting you, Aidan. Remember, I'm watching you!"

"Be careful," Magnolia yells at her back.

"Sure thing, Mom!"

"Don't talk to strangers," Magnolia adds.

"Strangers shouldn't be your worry," I whisper. "Boys she knows already are the problem." I grin.

Magnolia swats me on the shoulder. "Do I need to remind you that I was younger than she is when I got pregnant with her? I have every right to worry about every boy in the world. Strangers or not."

"I've never been more acutely aware of that fact now that I've met her. She is a carbon copy of you. I'm sorry. She seems to have a good head on her shoulders. Don't worry. Too much," I add. Magnolia turns to watch Kendall pedal her bike away. "That must have been hard. Giving up your childhood like that. So quickly."

"It wasn't easy," Magnolia says. "But I'd do it again if given the chance. She's everything to me."

"I know," I say. "You are doing a good job, Magnolia. In case no one has told you that lately. She went to bat for you against me because she cares about you."

She turns. "Thank you for saying that. Sometimes I think I can't do anything right by her."

Taking her waist, I bring her closer. "Don't think that for a second. I'd be happy to call you 'Mom.'"

"Aidan, that's weird as hell."

I chuckle. "I know. But you smiled, and that made it worth it."

"I read these articles that say once you divorce that the child should be the only focus, that parents having other relationships just ruins the kids even more. That was my worry, you know? That her seeing me with another man might trigger something and make her even more miserable."

"I'm not Paul, Magnolia. Kendall knows that. Do you?"

Her glassy eyes pool, and a tear slips. "I've never been more acutely aware of a fact in my life," she says, using my words. "I didn't expect happiness ever again. Especially by using a dating app. It feels like a dream."

I kiss her lips. She tastes like vanilla. My dick responds, but I pull away before I get too carried away. "Dream about me tonight."

"Banging me up against a wall?" Magnolia adds, pecking my lips with hers once more.

I press my lips into a firm line. "I meant something more sweet and romantic, but you went ahead and took it there, so yes. My lips on your neck. You moaning into my ear. My body filling yours. An orgasm or two that makes your legs tingle. Me coming inside you. It dripping down your legs and onto the floor. Me kissing you. Putting you to bed. Dream of that."

"Well, that sure gives me a vivid visual," she says, breathing heavily.

"I should go before it's a reality instead of a dream."

Magnolia nods. "Did you mean what you said about the best part?"

I lay both hands on the sides of her cheeks. "You are my best part, Magnolia."

She smiles, and another tear falls.

I wipe it away with my thumb.

The work meeting was tiresome, and there's a possibility I might have to head to San Diego for some medical studies they do on SEALs every so often. San Diego is still the main base that houses the bulk of our specialized facilities. It would just be for a week or so, but the thought of leaving Magnolia makes me uneasy. It's foreign. The attachment—this tug on my heart that's never been there before.

"You've been busy lately, man," Mercer drawls from an old leather chair in our rec room at work. There is a bar in here, and we eat lunch here some days. Photos of our brothers killed in action line the walls, and awards and news articles of our accomplishments are tacked on the wall with haphazard care. It's a man cave to the extreme. It smells a little like sweat and gunpowder. Someone is cleaning a gun on the counter behind me.

Tahoe walks in and slinks into a chair next to me. "He's got a lady now. My, how things change, am I right?"

I hate that he's right. Hate the years I spent naysaying, calling coupled dudes pussies. Quite the opposite is actually factual. Being in a relationship takes fucking balls. Huge ones. More nerve than is required to steal a life. It takes diligence. Persistence. Patience. Work. "You were right," I say, taking a sip of keg beer. "You heading to medical tomorrow too? I'm trying to get out of it."

"Yeah, I'll head over there. My back's been hurting," he says, rubbing his lower back. "Should have the specialists check that over." The sleek black boats we ride are torture on our bodies. We don't sit on them. We stand. And our spines take a beating as we speed on the wake. Most of the SEALs have some sort of lingering pain due to the trauma of our training. Hearing loss is common. So is back and neck pain. "You can't get out of it, dude. Might as well do it now."

"I know. I was just settling into small-town life. Heading back there won't be good for the mind, you know?" That's where all of my mistakes are buried. The women who I passed my time with. The failed relationship. The atmosphere that fostered a person I've walked away from.

Tahoe chuckles. "It will be different. Feel different. Plus, it's just for a week. Even Aidan Mixx can stay out of trouble for a week."

"I can," I affirm. Then I ask him about his life and listen to him talk about his family. I leave the conversation feeling a resolve—an unwavering commitment to the decision I've made about my future with Magnolia. It's a huge step, one I never in a million years thought I'd want to take. It's because I never met her. Never knew something this strong could exist.

I visit Magnolia at her store on my way home from work, and she locks the doors, and we ravage each other on a bare mattress upstairs twice before I finally leave for home. When I stopped in, it was to just say hello, and I told her as much, but I think that it stoked the flame even more because she jumped on me almost immediately. She wasn't happy when I told her I had to go to San Diego for a week, but she understood. Quality time with Kendall would never be a bad thing, she said, and there were a ton of activities going on at her high school that Magnolia could attend and help out with.

Just because she's okay with it doesn't mean I'm okay with leaving her. My apartment is silent and dark when I come in and throw my keys on the table—the blankets from our sleepover still on the floor. I slept there last night, too. It smells like her. It's safe. I shower and I'm about to turn on the television when I catch sight of a note on the countertop. It's written in Magnolia's girly script. It's an address. Somehow, and I'm not sure why, maybe it's my SEAL intuition, I know it's my parents' address. It didn't take her long to figure this one out.

Even though she has my best interests at heart, I'll never be able to face them again. My parents are near San Diego. Where I'll be for an entire week. They must have moved there recently. I wonder why they went there. It couldn't possibly be because that's where I was, so what was the reason? The address gives me enough to contemplate and to fill my brain with. I text Magnolia to tell her good night but make no mention of her note. I fall asleep in our love cocoon dreaming of the SoCal skyline. The dream swiftly morphs to fucking Magnolia against a wall. Her whispering that she loves me.

"Whoa, whoa, whoa, what are you talking about?"

Kendall is furious, standing in front of me in the kitchen. I came to say goodbye to Magnolia before I boarded the plane for San Diego. When I saw her busy in the garage, I decided to meander into the house for a drink of water. Obviously, a huge fucking mistake. Huge.

"He told me you are a player. That you're just using my mom. He told me you're going to leave her because she's too old. All you SEALs like them young," Kendall says, face tear-stained.

I hold up my palms. "Who said this?"

"That doesn't matter! It's true, isn't it?"

"It's not true. I've told you this before! Who told you that?" The panic sets in. I'm not equipped for this scenario. I have no idea what to say to calm a teenage girl. When Kendall first confronted me about this, I assumed it was town gossip. It's evident now that's not the case. "I love your mom."

"Bullshit. You're using her to get to me."

I swallow hard. Her father. The younger woman he had an affair with. Kendall is projecting her fears onto me. That's the only explanation. "Kendall, calm down. That's not true at all."

"I'm off-limits, so you're getting to me through her. That's what Leo said."

Anger. Seething red anger beats at my rib cage like an animal seeking freedom. "Leo told you that? What else did he say?" I'm going to kill the kid. Slaughter him like a goddamn enemy on the battlefield. He's miserable, and he's taking everyone down with him. The guy is a motherfucking grenade.

"I can assure you everything he said is false. Did he touch you?" Another breed of fury rears when I envision Leo doing anything untoward to Kendall. "Be honest with me."

Kendall looks away, out the window. "Don't do that," she yells.

"What?" I ask, my tone louder than I intended.

Her face wilts. "Pretend that you care about me." My heart breaks.

"I do care about you. I love you and your mother. This is it for me, kid."

She aims a finger at me like a gun. "You're such a liar. Like all men. Every one of you! All you do is lie!"

It takes a second or two for her accusation to settle in. For the horror and shock to take hold. I don't say anything.

"You want me."

I shake my head sadly. How fucked up is this? "Not like that, kid. Not like that."

"He told me so. I believe him," Kendall says, glancing quickly out the kitchen window. "And I'm going to help my mom now before it's too late. I want her all to myself, and I'm going to save her before this goes on any longer."

I furrow my brow. "What?" My anger is so permeating, I can't calculate her next move, and I should, because it's my job to predict others' actions. Love has fucked me up and down and every which way a person can be fucked.

The back screen door slams. *Magnolia.* Kendall throws herself into my arms, and I think she's hugging me. Like maybe she's upset and wants to be comforted by a father figure. She's distraught. That's not a leap, right? But then she twines her fingers into my hair and presses her mouth against mine.

What.

The.

Fuck.

Is.

Happening?

I put my hands against her shoulders, but my body

is shocked, unable to process what is taking place. I don't move my lips as Kendall's work against mine, in fact, I don't move a fucking muscle—not even to breathe.

"Aidan," Magnolia yells. "What the hell is going on?"

Her sweet, albeit broken, voice dashes the haze surrounding my body. I push Kendall away in a stiff, jerky movement. Facing Magnolia, I see the pain. The betrayal reflecting in her eyes. I see her reliving her worst nightmare once more. My stomach churns and my heart pounds.

"Magnolia. No. No," I plead. My voice sounds wrong. As if I'm outside, listening to someone else say the words. I see the sever—the disconnect—and I know nothing I'll say will matter. There is no witty joke or cocky swagger that can repair the scene she sees in front of her.

I swallow hard.

Fuck.

FOURTEEN

Magnolia

The hours blur into days, and the days blur into weeks and then a month. Then another. The intermittent chill of December is in the Florida air, and I'm a hollow shell of disbelief. I shut Aidan out completely. For only one reason: Kendall is getting better. She's happier than she's ever been now that my attention is solely focused on her. She confessed about her dalliance with an older teenager down at the beach, gave me very few details about him, but said he made her sad and confused. That was the reason she gave for the shared kiss. I had to accept it.

There are several voicemails on my cell phone pleading for a call back. I can't bring myself to delete them, I listen to them every night before I cry myself to sleep. Aidan showed up to my work a week after the kiss heard round the world. My heart skipped a beat, but then my brain delivered the bad news, and it stopped altogether for a beat or two.

Aidan is bad news. I knew it all along. A tiger can't change its stripes. He begged me to listen to him.

Pleaded on his knees, in fact. Told me a story about how some guy at his work poisoned Kendall's mind and told her lies. That Kendall kissed him because she knew I'd see it. She wanted to destroy the relationship because she thought he would hurt me in the end. He was tearful as he delivered his side of the story hoping I'd accept it…and him. Did I believe him?

I did. I think, anyway. But it didn't matter. Kendall adamantly denied the whole thing. Given the option of believing my daughter or believing Aidan, he has to know I'll always choose her side. I'll always choose her. What message would it send to Kendall if I said, "I know you're telling me that Aidan kissed you back and that you were confused and sad, but Aidan said something different, and I'm not only going to believe him, but I'm going to continue dating him?" Aidan refused to give me the name of the SEAL in question, and as much sense as it makes, I can't see Kendall entangling herself with someone that much older than herself. She knows better.

I'm cleaning the antique store, putting the finishing touches on the holiday window display which is a head tilt toward the Nutcracker ballet but formed entirely with small, ceramic trinkets. It's been a welcome distraction. My love life is in shambles. It's as if the universe said, "Here is your happily ever after, Magnolia. Just kidding. You don't get one of those."

Jenny comes in through the back door, her singsong greeting alerting me to company. "It's looking so good, Magnolia. How was your day?"

"Fine," I reply. "What brings you here? I told you yesterday, I'm fine. You can't just pop in all the time." Every other day, without calling first, Jenny is by my side.

"No, you put on the 'I'm fine' face and attitude for Kendall. I get that. You're definitely not okay, and I'm here so you can tell me every single way in which you're not fine."

I shake my head and clear a speck of dust off a mirror, which is acting as a skating pond. "I've been thinking a lot about that time he came here and told me his side of the story. It makes more and more sense as time passes, you know? I don't see any way around this. Kendall is happy." I say the last sentence because Jenny is a mother, and she will immediately know the magnitude of that. "She's even thinking of letting Paul visit her here. I'm not even sure if that's a good thing or not, but it's progress." I swallow hard. "I can't fuck everything up again. I'm too scared. I went out on a limb, and look what happened. It broke."

"It did. Snapped like a motherfucking twig, didn't it?" Jenny says. She sits down on a low stool next to me after locking the front door of Magnolia's Steals. "You do realize that's normal, right? Broken trees and all? Relationships tend to be a little messy."

"If you just came here for a pep talk or to make me feel bad about myself, you can just go."

Jenny groans. "You are such a drag these days. We have the fundraiser tonight, remember? I didn't want to wait to meet you at Betsy's because I have a name for you." I glare at my best friend, and she looks frightened, her eyes flaring wide. "I can't believe I'm breaking her trust like this, Magnolia. Don't make me regret it. I'm going to regret it. I wish I didn't overhear. I mean, I'm glad I overheard. Oh, shit. I don't know what I think anymore! I know the name of the boy Kendall was seeing. Down at the beach. The boy."

"Tell me," I yell, then cover my mouth. It came out

louder than I anticipated. I think I have an idea, but a name would give me something to go on and try to piece together this mess a little better.

"Now you want to be my friend. Jerk," Jenny says, eyes narrowed. "I was listening in the other night, and Kendall said something to Juliet about someone named Leo."

"Leo?" I furrow my brow. "I've never heard that name before. She's never brought him up. She said he was older, so maybe he's at the community college a couple of counties north?"

Jenny shrugs. "Not a familiar name to me either. I overheard her say it was who she was seeing when they biked down to the beach. It sounds like they might still be seeing each other."

"What? Fuck," I cry out, putting my face in both of my hands. Is that the real reason she's happy? Maybe her jubilant happiness has nothing to do with Aidan and me at all. Where the hell is the kid instruction manual when you need one? "What am I supposed to do, Jenny?"

"You find out who the hell this kid is, and you talk to him," Jenny says. "And you listen a little more specifically when the girls are talking at your house. About boys. Or the beach. Or anything remotely similar to those two things. You dig. You find the truth."

I don't want to spy. "I do need more information. What if Aidan was telling the truth?"

"Have you not considered that yet? I mean, to be honest, teenagers rarely tell the truth. You know that."

"My teenager tells the truth," I bite back.

Jenny holds up her hands. "Whatever you say. She tells the truth, but maybe she's omitting something important. You'd be naïve if you didn't assume that."

She's right. Jenny is telling the dirty truth. Now I'm tasked with snooping and hoping Kendall doesn't catch me. If she finds out, the trust will be broken forever. The possibility of having two untrustworthy parents is something I can't contemplate. Sighing, I drag my hand through my tangled hair.

"Our appointment at Betsy's is in ten minutes. Hair, nails. The works. You'll feel like a million bucks after. Grab your sweater, Magnolia. We're getting out of here. You don't have a choice. I get it. Believe her until you figure out who that kid is. Move on."

It's solid advice. It's advice I would have adhered to several months ago. Now that I know what moving on looks and feels like, I'm stuck in this place filled with memories and regret. I'm not sure I'll ever fully recover from Aidan Mixx.

We walk the block to Betsy's, and Jenny tells me about her last date with Harry. It's so simple in the most mundane way possible. I wonder if that's how she wants it, or if that's where the comfort zone lies. There's no passion or fierce desire to be with him when they're apart. She dates him once or twice a month, and they rarely talk in between.

"Do you love him?" I ask, turning to meet her gaze.

She wrinkles her nose. "Why would you ask that?"

"Because you've been seeing him for so long. Do you want to take the next step with him?"

Jenny scoffs. "Magnolia, please. Don't fix what's not broken. It works."

I bite my tongue. Is the sex good? Does her whole body tingle when he kisses her? Does she miss him? None of that matters. It's obvious she's chosen what she wants in life. Would that change if she knew that out there somewhere in the world was a man who would turn her life upside down? Make her feel things she didn't know were possible? Or is that too much of a risk? Having something so meaningful only to lose it? Having the rest of your life missing what you once had?

I nod in agreement, and we enter the beauty shop.

I can't remember the last time I styled my hair, so when the young girl spins me around in my chair to face the mirror, it takes a beat or two to adjust to my reflection. My brown hair is blown and curled at the ends, and my face has a smooth layer of makeup that brings out my blue eyes. "Thanks, it looks great," I say, fingering my hair.

"You look like a total babe," Jenny says, paying Betsy. I hand her cash so she can pay for mine too. "What are you going to wear?"

I shrug.

"You haven't picked something out yet?"

"I spent so much time trying to find Kendall a dress. She's the one on the Princess Court. What I wear isn't important. No one is going to be looking at me."

Betsy tsks at me. "That's the wrong attitude to take, honey. Men are always looking. It just might be the night the right man looks your way."

Sighing, I agree even if I don't believe it for a second. Jenny covers a laugh with a cough, and we leave for my house. Juliet and Kendall are waiting for a ride when we pull in. Both girls are in their sparkly gowns with painted faces and hair falling in curls. They look older than they actually are, and my heart skips a beat. Kendall as a woman is something to behold. An adult man would be blind to not find her attractive, regardless of her innocence and her barely underage status. I close my eyes and try to shut out my accusations.

"You look beautiful, sweetie," I say. I dropped her off at home after school, and she's been getting ready ever since. "I love your makeup and hair. The dress looks perfect."

"Thanks, Mom," Kendall squeals. "Juliet helped with my makeup. Do you think it's too much?"

A wistful smile forces its way to my lips. "It's perfect."

"You look so pretty, too," Kendall says, her smile falling. Her gaze darts to Jenny. "You guys have hot dates tonight?"

Jenny laughs. "Just trying to bring up her spirits, Kendall. Your mom is my hot date. What do you say, Magnolia? You coming home with me tonight? A sleepover? All night?"

"Ew, Mom, that's disgusting," Juliet says, wincing. "We need to go. We're supposed to be there early to get our jobs for the fundraiser. They're going to auction the Princess Court for ice cream dates! I hope one of the hot guys buys my date."

Jenny perches her hands on her hips and glares at her daughter.

I was so caught up in Juliet that I didn't see Kendall staring at me, hard. Studying me like a textbook she needs to memorize.

"Are your spirits down?" Kendall asks quietly, leading me to the car by my elbow.

"No, sweetie, Jenny was just being Jenny. Nothing is wrong," I reply. "I promise," I say, meeting her crystal-blue gaze, the same as my own.

"You'd tell me if you were upset, right? About

Aidan and everything that happened?" she says, and her eyes do that thing they used to do. The haunt. The memories are flooding in, no doubt. "You've seemed so happy."

I lay a hand on her cheek lightly, careful not to disturb her makeup. "I am happy." I smile, but I'm sure she notices it doesn't reach my eyes.

Kendall nods. This was my time to bring it up. To ask her again about Aidan's story and if there's anything she has to tell me, but I'm a chicken, too scared to rock the boat of Kendall's delicate stability.

Jenny drives the girls to the school while I waft through my closet halfheartedly. Jeans. I should wear jeans and a T-shirt and call it a day. At least my head looks pretty. The rest of me can be comfortable to even it out. My fingers land on the delicate blue dress I've never worn. I hold it out, look at the tags that are still attached, and decide to at least try it on.

It was game over when Jenny got back to pick me up and I was wearing the dress. She insisted I wear it. It's loose, but it also exposes small sections of skin. It's not too scandalous yet still comfortable, so I agree, and we leave.

We walk into the town hall, a big white building that has changed very little over the decades. The interior is already filled with music and laughter when we enter. There are vendors set up, and a band is playing low on the stage as waiters and busboys ready the tables for the fundraiser dinner. Jenny and I bought our seats as soon as they went on sale. The organizers chose where you will sit. We find our table cards and make our way through the bodies to the cash bar.

I can smell dinner from the nearby kitchens as I tell the bartender to go heavy on the vodka in my mixed drink. When Jenny gives me a look, I say, "You're my date tonight, right? You're sleeping with me. The least you can do is drive me home first." The guy pouring the drink looks uncomfortable as he hands me my drink. I pay him and throw a bill in his tip jar and grin at my friend as I turn from the bar.

That's when I see the uniforms. I've never seen so many of them together. A sea of black suits with ribbons littering their chests. They've taken over two of the tables in the large dining hall, their voices loud and boisterous as they talk to each other and survey the room around them, smiles wide and presence demanding. They're striking, and realization dawns. He's here.

"Fuck," I whisper under my breath. Jenny comes up beside me and links her arm with mine. "Did you know they were going to be here tonight? Don't lie." My voice shakes.

"I didn't know for sure, but come on, Magnolia, this is a small town. You don't think the mayor would want to show them off given the chance? The SEALs in Bronze Bay are like his prized ponies." She clears her throat. "I assumed they would be here, though."

"Thanks for reminding me about this earlier. I appreciate it."

She shrugs and pulls us toward our table, but I can't keep my gaze from wandering—from seeking Aidan out. "We're going to have a good dinner, and then we will go home, and the high school benefits from it. You know how badly they need the new gymnasium." Jenny is trying to distract me by giving facts.

"This is awful," I say, taking a large draw out of my drink and coughing when I taste the strong vodka.

"I can't stay here. I've been good at avoiding him this long, there's no reason that can't continue."

Juliet bounds up to us. "Can I have some money?" she asks her mom.

"For what?" Jenny sighs out.

"The SEALs are selling T-shirts for our fundraiser, and I want one," she says proudly.

My breath lodges in my throat. My worlds are mixing. This was never supposed to happen. In my mind, I'd be able to dutifully ignore Aidan until he moved away. Far away. Never to be seen or heard from again. That request would make my life too easy, obviously. My chest aches when Juliet snatches the twenty-dollar bill from her mother's hands and bounces away. I follow her with my gaze to the T-shirt table and I see Kendall. She's talking to a uniformed man, her grin wide and if her lashes batted any faster, she'd take flight.

I don't even pause to consider the consequences. Marching toward my daughter, my mind is on only one thing. Getting her away. Saving her.

"Kendall," I say, breathless. She turns to me with wide eyes. Deer in the headlights.

"Mom," she replies. "Uh," she mumbles. "Can I buy a T-shirt?"

I clear my throat, looking at the man she's talking to. He's tall, broad like his friends, but unlike his friends, he has a different air, and a more devious aura seeps from his body. Also, he is so much younger. "Introduce me to your friend."

The man smiles. My stomach sinks. He extends his hand. "I see where Kendall gets her beauty from." His tone drips with sarcasm. "I'm Leo Callaway."

Leo. Leo. Leo. It connects. Kendall must read it on

my face. Or she's intuitive enough to know she's in trouble after all of this time. "No," I say, taking my hand from his. "You can't buy a T-shirt, Kendall. Go sit at my table next to Jenny right now. I need to talk to Leo."

Kendall doesn't say a word. She leaves quickly, her heels clicking as she finds her way to Jenny. My breathing quickens. My pulse hammers. I see red. When I'm confident Kendall is safely with Jenny, I meet Leo's gaze.

"Looking for your ex-boy toy?" Leo slides in, licking his lips.

"Excuse me?" I say, furrowing my brow.

"He decided on something a little younger. Sally?" Leo says, tapping his chin like a condescending asshole. "No, wait." He snaps. "Polly. That's it. Polly. He's probably fucking her in the bathroom again. I can't believe he tapped your old pussy for so long. We all like them young. Everyone knows that." His nefarious gaze flits over to Kendall.

My stomach sinks, and my brain does that funny swimming thing that happens before I faint. It's only happened once before, many years ago. I steady myself on the table next to us and take several deep breaths. Leo walks away, cackling under his breath.

"Is that little asshole bothering you, Mrs. Sager?" A low, Southern voice rolls over me.

"I'm fine," I say, keeping my face down.

He clears his throat, so I force myself to acknowledge the voice. It's Aidan's friend, Mercer. He smiles a lopsided grin. "Don't believe anything he says. He's been fighting with Aidan for months. Rabid. Fucking. Fighting. Are you sure you're okay, ma'am?"

I'm not okay. "Don't call me ma'am. Or Mrs.

Sager. I'm not married. It's Magnolia!" I scream, and people turn to gawk at me. "Is he with Polly?" I choke on the name of the girl who came to his house the first night I was there. The memory is hazy because it has been replaced with good things, but it's funny how much I overlooked at the start. Why? Because his touch felt like magic. Because his words were a salve to my soul. Because I fell in fucking love with the devil himself.

Mercer looks uneasy. "I'm sorry, Magnolia. I didn't mean any offense," he drawls, holding up two palms. "Can I get you anything?"

"Answer my question," I growl.

He glances away toward the table of SEALs and then back toward me. "I don't know," he whispers. "I don't know what game Leo is playing at, but it's dangerous."

Mercer walks away and leaves me alone in a crowded room, my body turned inside out. Others have to be able to sense my vulnerable state, it has to be on display. It shouldn't affect me. Aidan has moved on. Or moved back to his old ways. I was a fool to believe I'd changed him. I was merely another stop on his whore train to pound town. I bet he does the falling act for every woman. It's how he hooks them. Makes himself seem like an honorable, desirable candidate.

Mercer may not know what game Leo is playing at, but I'm about to find out. Not for myself, no. For my daughter.

FIFTEEN
Aidan

San Diego—Two Months Ago

There had to be a point in falling in love. A lesson learned. Something to be gained by feeling this pain. The address was crumpled in my pants pocket. I'd already memorized it, I kept it because it's in her handwriting. It's how I'm hanging on to the impossible. I vomited in Magnolia's front yard before making my way to the airport to head here. The scenario plays over and over anytime I close my eyes. I haven't slept. I'm barely eating. Not only won't Magnolia pick up my calls, I know she never will. Not after seeing the strength of a mother-daughter bond for myself. That is sacred. An outsider is what I'd always be.

I finished all of my medical tests at noon. Before I knew what I was doing, or why, I ended up parked in front of their house—in a nondescript middle-class neighborhood. It's the kind of neighborhood bad guys hide in. The kind so plain and unappealing new people rarely move in and residents never move away. It's a prison. An illusion of security with a hard edge that only I can feel.

There are no cars in the driveway, but I know my father always parks his vehicles inside the garage. A fact I doubt time changed. I get out of my rental car and survey the area with a keen eye. I wait, but the dread doesn't come like I assumed it would. A sense of relief washes over me, and I hate that she's right. That she's won another piece of me I'll never get back. I need this.

Pacing slowly, I don't think about what I'll say if they're home, only seeing them, letting them see me. A whole, self-made man. Sure, I've arrived today as a man who has nothing to lose, but this journey began on completely different terms—back before I lost everything.

I can be a man worthy. Magnolia showed me that. It has to be the takeaway. There's no other logic I can wrap my brain around when I think about the time we spent together and what she taught me. I ring the doorbell once and wait. She opens it, and I see the second her confusion turns to sorrow—regret. The years have been kind to her, the lines on her face deeper than they were when I was a child. Her hair is gray, and the frown lines around her mouth are deep and telling. Happiness never lived inside her.

"Aidan, son, is that you? Oh my gosh, get in this house right now and give your mama a hug," she croons, voice creaky from disuse.

I laugh. "You want a hug?" I choke out. "You want a hug," I repeat, shaking my head, motherfucking tears already threatening. "Is he home?" I ask.

She looks down at her feet and shakes her head. "He died, son. Five years ago."

I try to swallow, but it's lodged in my throat, along with my breath. I hold it in for several more seconds before I blow it out, rough and noisily. "Jesus," I whisper, as my legs give out. I sit right there on the cement in front of the door and put my face in my hands.

She leans over and puts a hand on my back. I jerk away. "I tried to get in touch with you, but the Navy wouldn't give me the information. I'm sorry, son." Every time she calls me "son," my skin prickles. There's a reason they wouldn't give her the information. I told them not to. "He was so proud of what you made of yourself, Aidan. You should know that. Every single day he prayed for your safety. Prayed you'd find your way home to us so that he could shake your hand. You did it."

Emotion floods her voice, and it's the last straw. A traitorous tear slides against the palm pressed to my face.

I'm not angry. I'm not confused. I'm furious with sadness. "I did do it," I say, looking up at her. The same position I was in my entire childhood. "All by myself," I call, shaking my head. "Not because of anything he did. Because of the man I made myself."

Her eyes glaze over. "I know we were awful parents. I know, son. We weren't sure how to make sure you grew up successfully. We didn't know. I'm sorry. Your father was sorry. But look," she says, tears streaming down her face. "You are a hero. A strong, brave hero."

"Not because of you," I deadpan. "Despite you. You guys were fucked up. Think how strong and brave I'd be if you actually loved me."

"Is that what you think? That I didn't love you?"

she asks, letting the door close and sitting down in front of me so I have to meet her sad gaze.

"You let him beat me. For no reason at all. What made you think that was okay? That's not love," I growl. "And the reason I know that is because I tasted pure love for the first time, and I know exactly what it is. It's why I'm here. Why I came to show you that I'm a person worthy of being loved. I am a hero, but not for the obvious reasons. You know why? Because I survived you."

She covers her mouth with a weathered hand as her eyes crinkle in pain. "Son," she sobs.

I continue on. "I survived you, and I soldiered on. I got a little mixed up, and sometimes I did horrible things to people because I had to learn how to treat people I care about the hard way. No one ever cared about me. How the fuck was I supposed to know how to have a relationship? My sole role models for a family unit were completely neglectful and abusive. I succeeded in my career, and everything else around me crumbled. Then I met her. It was a revelation. A goddamn stroke of luck." I think of Magnolia, and my chest aches. "I fucked it up, because what choice did I have? A man like me doesn't deserve that kind of love, right? Fuck me."

"That's not true, and you know it. If that woman loves you like you love her, then choices aren't a factor. There is no choice to be made. Love forgives, Aidan. Weak men blame their pasts for their mistakes. Nobody is perfect."

I sigh a haggard breath. "I'm not blaming you. I just want to know why you never tried to save me."

"You didn't need saving. You were a strong boy."

I bark a laugh. "I was a child."

"I was wrong," she says, taking my hand in hers. I can't find it in me to pull away. "Your father and I were both wrong. I'm so sorry you endured a less-than-ideal childhood. I loved you. I love you still. When you have a child, you'll understand what that kind of love feels like. The balance is hard. Forming an adult while loving a child. I wasn't tender enough. You deserved more from me, and I failed you." She sucks in a breath that seems strong enough to rattle her rib cage. "He beat me too. Your father beat me too. That was my normal. Our normal."

I stay quiet. I never expected this conversation. An apology. My whole adult life was formed because of miscommunication, or rather, the thought that I was strong so I didn't need culpable love in physical form. Their way of loving me was their own. Can I respect that while disagreeing completely? Her hand squeezes my own, a reminder that he's gone and she's here. A mother hoping to reconnect with a son. I'd give anything for another chance with Magnolia. To be in her proximity. To feel her lips against mine. If her love would be mine again, I'd be able to face this. Alone? I don't know if I'm strong enough.

I run a hand through my hair. "I'll leave you my phone number. I'm living in Florida now. A small town called Bronze Bay. I'm heading back there in a few days after I finish up some testing here." I stand, helping her up as I go, grabbing her other hand. I see the frailty then, the way she wobbles without me as leverage. "You live here by yourself?"

"A nurse comes to check in once a week, but I'm used to it. Since your father died, I've found peace in being alone. No one to worry about except myself." She rubs her neck as she speaks, the loneliness creeping into her tone. "I don't want to talk about myself. Tell me about you. Tell me everything. If this is my one chance to see you, I'm taking it. Give me everything you can. All the good and the bad." She holds open the screen door, and her arm shakes a bit.

Something cracks, a weakness in my armor. This isn't what I planned on, but I know without a doubt it's what Magnolia hoped would happen. I swallow hard and sigh, reaching out to hold the door for her, I say, "Okay, Mom."

She turns back, beaming. I return the smile. I can't mete out forgiveness to my father, but perhaps my mother is deserving.

I deleted the dating apps off my phone the night after I returned from San Diego and tried to talk to Magnolia at her shop. She ordered me out without even considering my truth. It's what I expected. What I didn't expect was to feel so downtrodden because of it. No one tells you how awful a breakup is. What confuses me is how quickly the person you love the most in the world turns into a complete stranger in a short amount of time. I see her from a distance when she's closing the store, and it's as if I'm watching a person I don't know. The Magnolia Sager that came after we ended. Another human.

Leo has been making my life a living hell since the breakup, taunting some pseudo relationship-slash-friendship with Kendall over my head. Others swear to me he hasn't touched her, but my anger refuses to accept that. She's a kid. And she's mine. I've broken his nose once, given him two black eyes, and threatened to end his life if they didn't ship his ass to Cape Cod as soon as humanly possible. His orders are in, and he's leaving next month, so I've backed off, but I still keep tabs on the fucker for Magnolia's sake. I'm responsible for Leo being in their world to begin with. I recall the conversation on the beach when I told him that Magnolia was off-limits. Why would I think to add Kendall into that spoken order? Never in my wildest dreams did I think he would move in this sneaky, desperate way. He hasn't done anything illegal, so no actions can be taken. Being friends with a teenager isn't a crime, especially when you are a teenager yourself. It's hard when two years difference is close to nothing once you're in an adult relationship. I don't want to accept that intellect now. Not when it affects me and those I love.

I brush my sweaty hair off my face and mop it with my T-shirt. The gym is empty, and I'm thankful I don't need to make small talk with anyone. Tonight we have a mandatory fundraiser for the local school district. We have to be there, and I'd rather be anywhere else besides in a room with Leo, but I was told there isn't an option. Sighing, I hit the showers and put on my dress uniform. I fix my hair, leave the office, and put my cover on. It's a short walk to Town Hall, and it's already buzzing with people. I see my brothers right away and make sure Leo isn't in sight before approaching the group.

Mercer slaps my shoulder. "Got that extra workout in, bro?"

I nod. "Three times today." I'm not fucking, so I need the adrenaline release and endorphins working out gives me. Bonus points because it clears my mind, and it's the only time, all day, that happens.

He cups my arm. "Your muscles are even more perfect than they were before. I want to hump them."

I push him away, shaking my head. "Is the fucker here?"

"Oh, he's here, but he's staying out of the way. He knows he's not welcome in the crew. It's so fucked up what he did to you, man. We all agree." Mercer shoves a beer into my hand. "Oh, there was someone looking for you, though." His pink cheeks tell me he's been drinking for quite a while already, and his grin is mischievous.

My heart skips. "Magnolia is here?" My voice changes when I say her name, and he catches it.

"No, no, man. Sorry. Didn't mean to get your hopes up."

The elation quickly turns to dread as I sip the beer. I need to stop that. Getting all bent dicked over Magnolia when she clearly wants nothing to do with me. "Polly was looking for you. Heard you were single again," Mercer explains, glancing away so he doesn't have to witness my pain.

"Wonder who she heard that from," I deadpan, scanning the crowd for my nemesis. "That kid is trying to fuck me over constantly. I never did anything to piss him off."

Mercer clears his throat. "He's the kind of guy who doesn't need a reason."

I brush a piece of lint off my jacket. "Where is Polly?"

Mercer's drunk smile appears again. "Atta boy. Get back in the saddle. She was in the foyer looking for her table number when I last saw her. She's wearing some weird flowery dress or some shit. It's short."

I clap him on the back and excuse myself. I take off my cover when I enter the building and look at the main desk where table numbers are being issued. Polly isn't there, but Magnolia and Jenny are walking away, toward the bar. I trip over my own feet and have to steady myself on the doorframe. She's so beautiful—the low lights falling on her bare shoulders like an invitation. I'd give anything to kiss them again. She saunters with confidence as she talks to the bartender. My brothers filter in and move toward two tables in the center of the dining room.

I move away from them, heading toward the sign for the restrooms. It's a hallway I can hide in for a second. While my mind flits through all of the possible outcomes of me saying hello, Leo rounds the corner. He winks at me when he enters the restroom. I follow him in.

"You need to fucking watch yourself, Leo. You're playing with fire. You might be getting transferred, but you're pissing off a lot of people. That's not good for business. You're new to the Teams, so let me be the one to say, you are only one indiscretion away from being fired completely." I mean it to sound like a threat. I am his senior, but he knows enough that I alone would be hard-pressed to have him fired without solid, indisputable evidence.

He pisses into the urinal and tilts his head back, eyes closed. "I don't know what you're talking about. I haven't touched Kendall. We're just friends."

"Bullshit," I scoff. "Stay the fuck away from them. This isn't a game. This is their life."

He zips his fly and readjusts his cock. "Not a

game? Life is a game, brother. Have a good night." He winks at me as he leaves, and I'm left holding fury and jealousy.

I slide down the filthy wall until my ass hits the ground. I don't know how long I stay in here trying to come up with a plan that will backfire on Leo and expose the truth, but I snap directly out of it when Polly slides into the men's room and flattens her back against the door.

"He said you wanted me to meet you in here?" Polly whispers. "Is that true?" I don't know if it was Mercer, who was trying to do a good thing, or Leo, who is trying to set me up, but in this moment I don't have any fucks left to give. I stand up.

She stalks toward me, her ass hanging out of the cheap dress she poured herself into. When she's in front of me, I take her hands in mine. "Listen," I say, swallowing hard, "Polly, I want to apologize for being an asshole."

Her face changes, and her head tilts to the side in confusion. "I forgive you," she mumbles.

"I was a bad man." I sigh. "I did a lot of bad things to people who didn't deserve it. I'm trying to be better now." I lean over and kiss her cheek just as Magnolia blows in the door.

"Oh my god, this chick again?" Polly hisses. "She has a radar on you or something! I thought you were finished with her. That's what you said."

"I never said that," I clap back, gently moving Polly out of the way. "Magnolia," I plead. "Please, talk to me. Please."

She nods. "I don't care that you're in here fucking Polly, Aidan. Trust me. They told me this is where you'd be." Magnolia glances at Polly and back to me.

"I'm resigned to the fact that you will always be the same."

"He's not fucking me," Polly says, folding her arms across her chest and yanking on her hem. Magnolia's gaze darts to the dress.

She rolls her eyes. "Yeah. Sure. We both know Aidan Mixx is a skirt chaser, and yours looks just his style."

I clear my throat. "I'm not fucking Polly." I enunciate each word.

Magnolia holds her palms up, shaking her head. "I need you to tell me everything about Leo. Right this second."

"Why? What happened?" I ask, taking a step toward her. She's so fucking beautiful I can't help myself. I'm drawn to her. My skin prickles with awareness. Polly huffs out a string of curse words and leaves us. Magnolia locks the door, and my dick jerks. It's still on love autopilot—doesn't know that's not what a locked door means anymore.

"Is he with Kendall?" Magnolia asks, biting her lip to control the quivering. "He is so young. I should have known."

I put my hands in my pockets and look at the floor. Her pain isn't something I'm prepared to deal with tonight. Not again. Not ever again. Not at my expense, at the very least. "I've been keeping tabs, and everyone says he's not with her. Like that. But I don't know for sure. I'm sorry. Other than him focusing on ways to ruin my life, I don't know anything else."

Her breathing turns ragged, and she cries out. My feet react before my brain determines the right course of action, and she's folded in my arms and sobbing into my chest in the next second. "He said he likes them young. Says you all like them young. Kendall was looking at him," she says, hiccupping, "like she knows him. Really knows him, Aidan. I don't know what to do."

"I already did all that needs to be done, Magnolia. He's being sent to the Cape Cod base in less than a month. Until then I'll be on him like white on rice. He won't get near her. I promise you, okay? I'm handling this."

"Why are you being so kind to me?" she whispers. Pressing a kiss against her head, I inhale her scent like a dying man's last breath. I don't care if she realizes I'm taking her in like oxygen. It's a desire so strong I don't have control over it. I need a fix.

She pulls away, and her glassy blue eyes are so stunning I have to close my own to compose myself. Being this close to her without having permission to have all of her is a brand of torture even I wouldn't condone. "Magnolia. It was the truth. Everything I said before. It wasn't some twisted lie to get you back. I'm sorry. I know it doesn't change anything because Kendall has to come first. I understand. Maybe someday in the future when Kendall is ready to reveal the whole story, we can make something again. I'll wait for you, but I can't be the bad guy stuck between you two. Not when the only person I want to be for you and her is the good guy. The hero. The one who saves you. I'd never do anything to jeopardize our relationship. Leo is a bad kid who has infiltrated a battlefield he had no right to fight in."

She wipes underneath her eyes to clear the watery black tears. "I need to talk to her. We need to talk to her, Aidan. I'm not promising anything because as much as I love you, I have to love her more." The reason I love her is part of the reason I may never have her again.

"But you love me," I say, smirking a bit at the words dancing in my head. She still loves me. "I've gotta grasp onto something."

She shakes her head sadly. "I'm going to talk to Kendall and bring her to the shop to show her the window display tonight. Meet me at Magnolia's Steals in a few hours. With you there, she might open up. Maybe she'll be forced to tell the truth." I can hear the heartbreak in her voice, and I don't want to know what that battle feels like. The love for a man versus the love for her child.

"And yes," she says, interrupting my thoughts. "Of course I love you. Even if you bang bimbos in a men's restroom. Obviously I am beyond helping. I'm a desperate breed of a doormat."

I grab her chin. "You are not a doormat. I was not having sex with Polly. I was apologizing to her for being an asshole in my former life. I haven't been with any women since you, and I don't want to be with any other woman except you. You are the end-all, be-all to women for me. You're it. The only one." The urge to press my mouth against hers rises. Leaning in, I get close, she even closes her eyes in wait, but I pull away. "You're not mine, so I'm not going to kiss you." She's so near I can taste her breath and scent her skin. My head swims. My cock stiffens. I imprint this as a moment of pure torture and bliss wrapped into one.

She pulls away, wipes her eyes once more, and unlocks the door. The magic moment is broken. I didn't think I'd have this chance again to share this close space.

"Three hours? Please?" she asks. "No promises."

I nod once, stoic. "I'll be there."

The sky-blue dress floats behind her as she leaves. Her perfume lingers in the air, and facing the mirror, I see my jacket and dress shirt have smears of her makeup along the collar. Fuck, what am I doing? I tear out of the restroom and head for the bar for a stiff drink and then to my table. I try to make small talk with my brothers, but I always let my gaze find Magnolia and Kendall. In three hours, I have to convince a teenager to tell the truth. The rest of my life depends on it.

Talk about mission impossible.

SIXTEEN

Aidan

Leo is nowhere to be found for the next couple of hours. Mercer and Colton are talking about the Harbour Point SEAL base and how the initiative to get guys to transfer there has been incentivized with a huge bonus. My only thought is I hope Leo doesn't get it. Rarely are there SEALs who rock the boat as much as Leo. Sometimes bad seeds slip through the cracks and make it through BUD/S. Whoever sat on the panel and said yes to Leo should be fired.

Kendall and Magnolia left the fundraiser at the same time. Both were visibly upset—a fight surely brewing between them as they walked into the night. I check my watch several different times as time ticks slowly when I'm forced to be somewhere I don't want to be. The mayor comes over and thanks us for our attendance, and we all pretend we're having the best time and thank him for the invitation. We are his show ponies for the evening, and we all know it. We're left to recite rehearsed stories to a few people the mayor is entertaining, and at the stroke of ten, our commitment ends.

Tahoe and a few of the other married guys stay, dancing with their wives, happy to have a date night to themselves. The rest of us take off, melting into the crowd and skulking toward the exit. Mercer and Colton are heading to Bobby's Bar and ask if I want to join them. I give them a solid maybe, as it will depend on how my conversation with Magnolia goes, and head back to the base to pick up my truck. Polly is waiting out front at the guard shack in front of the compound. She's unable to get further without a military badge or without having her name on the guest list.

"What's up, Polly?"

"That's all you had to say? You really just wanted to apologize to me tonight? Nothing more?" In the dim light of the streetlights, I can see that she's upset. "I thought maybe we could have another night together. Or more."

This is irritating. In the vein of not being a cocky asshole, I decide to give her the time of day, or in this case, night. "Come on," I growl, showing the guard at the shack my ID and vouching for Polly. He smiles and waves me on.

"I really did miss you. As awful as you treated me, I know we had something special."

Do it like a Band-Aid. Rip it off fast, Aidan.

"I'm in love with Magnolia. I really was apologizing because no one deserves to be cast off that way. I'm sorry if you were led to believe this was happening." I motion between our bodies with one fluid gesture. "It's not."

She shakes her head sadly. "What does she have that I

don't? She has a kid. An ex-husband. More baggage than can be contained in the pit of an airplane. Help me understand." Polly crosses her legs, and suddenly it strikes me how much confidence she lacks. I was too concerned with sex and release to know her. To know any of them.

We're outside, so my cover is still on, but I raise it a bit so she can see my eyes. "It has nothing to do with you," I explain. "You're fine. You're perfect. Just not for me. It has nothing to do with her baggage, and her parental status isn't of any concern." I lay my fist against my chest. "Trust me on this, Polly. You want a man to want you more than anything else in the world. To be indisputably, unfailingly his. You want to be imprinted on his heart and in his mind so severely that there's no question. You are his person." I sigh, emotionally exhausted. I wasn't prepared for sadness. I thought she might smack me again, and I'd tear out of the parking lot and head for Magnolia's Steals. This is taking longer than I thought it would.

A few other men filter through the gate and head toward the parking lot where we're at. I wrap my arm around her shoulder and guide her back to the guard shack. As we walk, she asks, "And you feel that for Magnolia? Leo sent me here. Told me you'd be here. I just wanted to hear it for myself." Why would he send her here?

Blowing out a frustrated breath, I reply, "Yes. One hundred percent yes. Even if I shouldn't feel that way —have no right. She's my person whether she wants to be or not. I'll live with it. I'll always love her in every way."

"She's crazy if she doesn't work things out with you, Aidan Mixx. Certifiably insane," Polly whispers.

Turning out of my grasp, she makes her way to the

sidewalk on the other side of the road and waves before she disappears into the darkness. This dalliance with Polly has made me ten minutes late. Jogging back to my vehicle, I strip out of my jacket, toss my cover onto the passenger seat, and crank the engine.

The drive to the town center takes two minutes, but I know in one that something is very wrong. There is a tepid, thick smoke rising, and people are bustling on the sidewalk, pointing in the sky. In any other area of Bronze Bay, it would be someone burning their leaves, brush, or trash, but this smog is dark, and it is here, in the center of town. The smoke blows toward the ocean, and I pick up my pace, going more than ten miles per hour over the limit. It must be a pretty bad car accident to produce this much hazy darkness.

It hits me all at once, the scent is wrong. My guard is up when I park in the public lot closest to the town center. I jog down the sidewalk trying to find the source of the fire. The haze thickens as I get closer, and as I pass a café, I hear someone say, "It's the antique store. The whole thing is up in smoke!" Instead of slowing my pace to ask questions, I break out into a full-on sprint, dodging those passing by. I round the last corner, and my stomach drops, and my bones turn to ice. Magnolia's Steals is burning. There are sirens in the distance, people gawking, and heat. Inferno quality, motherfucking heat radiating from the building.

Surely they aren't in there. Waiting for me. This has been burning for at least fifteen minutes. Hopefully they weren't even here. My gaze darts to the window display, and the shawl that matched Kendall's dress is draped over a stool directly behind the scene displayed. They were there. Are still in there. I break back into a sprint and head for the back door. It's unlocked, so I wedge myself in the door and try to focus my gaze in the gray, swirling air. Someone screams, an ear-piercing, agonizing wail from upstairs. "Help!" The word is clear as day, and my stomach lurches as the worst-case scenario flits to awareness.

Pushing my emotions aside, I click into work mode. I tear off my button-up shirt and hold it over my face as I make my way to where the stairs were from memory. The fire is on the second floor of the building, and it's infiltrated the left half of the downstairs area. I turn the corner, and I see the door to the back room open. Magnolia is lying on the floor illuminated by a red light, hair floating around her like a halo, eyes closed. I run to her, kneeling beside her, and I pull her into my arms.

Magnolia blinks her eyes a few times, and they flutter open. "Fuck," I hiss. "I'm getting you out of here." Two things happen next. A supporting beam falls to the side, trapping Magnolia on the floor, her leg pinned at the ankle, and Kendall ruthlessly screams out for help from upstairs.

"Aidan," Magnolia croaks. "Please save her."

This is the nightmare. The one where I get to choose how I die. Slowly. Or quickly. I choose, no one else gets this honor. Like one of those video games where you get to pick your own adventure. Save the woman I love. Or kill the woman I love by letting her daughter suffocate in flames. I don't think my mother taught me much over the years, but recently I've discovered what it means to love a child. I'm pulling on the offending beam, trapping her, burning my palms, and listening to Magnolia choke on her pleas when I make the most selfless decision I've ever made in my life. I walk away from Magnolia Sager. I leave her near-lifeless body on the floor of a burning building, and I pound the creaky stairs to find Kendall. Her screams died off, and I'm anticipating the worst when I kick in the door to the spare bedroom where I first made love to Magnolia. I can't see through the smoke up here. It's cascading around me like a carnival ride of death. I cough and wheeze. I huff, and I get lightheaded.

"Help," Kendall croaks from somewhere close.

My knees hit the end of the bed, and I feel around for her and catch hold of an ankle and yank her toward me. Everything is hot. Too hot. My skin is crawling. I heave Kendall over my shoulder and cut the same path I came from, except the floor gives way and my leg falls through the feeble, burning hardwood.

Kendall stays on my shoulder, but the added weight sinks me farther. I can't breathe. She's not talking, and I doubt she's conscious by the limp weight on my shoulders. With a determination that comes from a place I've never tapped, I pull myself up and out of the floor. There is blood. There is a broken bone in my foot, too. I can feel the bite of pain and the wetness. The roof next to us collapses, and it rains down fire on our exposed skin.

Haphazardly, I wobble forward, because I know our time is limited. We're going to die here. All of us. The stairs aren't safe if the roof is caving in and support beams are falling. Flames lick up from every angle, but I make it down using the handrail and balance I didn't know I possessed. I blow out the front door and collapse into a heap on the sidewalk. Just Kendall and me.

Funny time for my lungs to give out now that they

finally have an oxygen source. The last thing I remember is someone putting an oxygen mask on my face and the fuzzy sight of Kendall being loaded into an ambulance. I'd tell someone to go get Magnolia, that I need to go back in, but my vocal cords don't work, and my brain can't form words.

No one knows she's in there burning alive.

Burning for love.

I come to in the hospital, with two men staring down at me—speaking words that echo before settling on the correct syllables. Nothing makes sense. Couldn't tell you if minutes have passed, hours, or days, only that my chest hurts and anytime I breathe, a pain slices my throat like a machete. I'm repeating one word on autopilot. "Magnolia." Or at least, that's what I'm trying to say, and I'm not sure they can decipher it with the mask on my face. I make a move to take off the mask, but they hold my arms down.

My muscles, those bastards I work so hard for, fail me when it matters most. The nurse's grip feels like a vise grip. I kick, trying to find purchase to sit up, but a new pain slides up my body, beginning on the left leg. A coolness spreads up my arm stemming from my elbow. Blackness overtakes my senses. In a half-dream, half-reality state, I envision another alternative to the disaster. When I run into the fiery house, I'm able to save them both because I didn't stop to talk to Polly, who wasn't a good guy. I tossed her a cocky one-liner about one-night stands, and I leave her in the dust. When I get to the antique store, I have time to tell

Magnolia how much I love her, and rescuing them both takes mere seconds. Heat doesn't exist in my dream scenario, neither does smoke that suffocates. It's just us and the simplicity of knowing we're all safe and will remain so for the rest of time. The knowledge of the lies I'm telling myself begins to prick the dream, like pinholes letting in light where it shouldn't be. More and more of the truths seep in. Horrible, life-altering truths I'm not sure how I'll live with. My body jerks, and I'm back in my dim reality, unable to accept the truth.

I have no gear. No fancy, cutting-edge armor to protect me in this mission. My brothers aren't standing by or covering my six. It's hard to make sense of what has happened when the loneliness haunts me so pervasively.

Magnolia is gone, and I'm the one who failed to save her.

SEVENTEEN
Aidan

It feels like the whole town is at her funeral. It's standing room only in the old Baptist Church. I lean my back against the wall, keeping my palms pressed on the chair rail to stay grounded, so I don't do anything stupid. My brothers are beside me, finally. We are a team, standing watch as the service rolls on. Kendall catches my eye briefly before dabbing a tissue against her eyes and refocusing her attention on the front of the church. My stomach lurches when I hear my name mentioned again. They call me a hero. A person in the right place at the right time. A brave, selfless man who saved Kendall's life. They said had I not taken her out of the building when I did, she wouldn't have made it —the smoke inhalation would have claimed her life. She recovered quickly, as young people tend to do, in and out of the hospital in a few days. As the speaker drones on, I turn my gaze to my feet, the left one in a brace from the foot sprain that I thought was a break in my smoke-induced haze. The words are meaningless when my soul is screaming *failure* every other heartbeat.

Saving Kendall wasn't enough. I am of the most elite class of individuals—so few can compete at my level. Not even professional athletes, and yet I couldn't save Magnolia. No one would ever dare ask me out loud. But I see the questions in their eyes. *You couldn't save them both? Why didn't you save them both? Why didn't you take Magnolia out of the shop and go back in for Kendall? You're a SEAL. You could have saved them both. Why? Why?* I won't say it was impossible, because if I had been on time, I could have had them out of there in no time flat. Blaming Polly got me nowhere. Blaming Leo didn't either. The string of decisions and choices led me there, at that time, on that fateful night, and we live with the consequences of our actions. Sometimes the consequences are far more severe than you'd expect. I'm used to life-and-death scenarios. This death takes away my breath, and I'm still waiting to get it back.

Everyone filters up to pay their last respects, filing into line in the center aisle. The same aisle used almost every Saturday in the summer for a white wedding. My feet feel like lead as I cut the same path as those before me. When it's my turn, the pastor smiles at me. "Thank you for your service, son. The world is better because you're in it."

My throat, which still aches when I swallow too much food, clogs with emotion. I shake his hand and nod instead of giving a verbal response. Faulty electrical wiring caused the fire. The window display was connected to an outlet that isn't typically used, and the heavy load was too much for the bad wire job. There is nothing left of Magnolia's Steals but for a pile of black ashes. The charred remnants are a painful reminder of everything Bronze Bay has lost.

There is a line of her crew to the right of the casket, and I shake hands with each and every firefighter in her unit. The unit that arrived on the scene of the fire at the same time I saved Kendall. The woman, Andrea Sinclair, the hero I couldn't be, saved Magnolia Sager and perished in the fire. A support beam fell directly on her head moments after she brought Magnolia to safety. It was tragic, and…it was my fault. I should have gotten Magnolia out of there before the beam fell on her.

"Thank you so much," I whisper, my voice a crackling, harsh grate. There was nothing from that night I remember after I collapsed, desperate for oxygen. These men and women before me took over. Truly saved the day…and Magnolia's life.

The last firefighter nods and shakes my hand, his face a grim representation of what he's lost. Gazing back at the coffin draped in the American flag, I'm struck with the memories of all the funerals I've attended in the past. Funerals for my brothers at arms. Deaths at the hands of bad guys, accidents, cancer, stray bullets in training, and explosions. Years and years of mortality that grind on my heart and steal my breath. This is no different. I thank Andrea once more, under my breath, for saving my heart, and then leave the church through the side door.

The attendees are mingling, sharing memories of the Bronze Bay Fire Department crew, friends and family passing happy memories of the fallen hero. I gravitate toward my men, the ones in the same uniform as me, and fall into conversation. They pat my shoulder and try their hardest to give just the right amount of empathy tinged with humor. Not too much because then they'll make me feel bad, too little and they're fucking jerks.

SEALs are known for their chameleon personalities. We're almost psychopaths. The keyword being *almost.* We are charismatic, type A, alluring perfectionists. We zone in on things that interest us, and we obsess. We are cutthroat in competition and can file away emotion like a mundane, everyday chore. It's borderline only because we don't possess the bad qualities true psychopaths harness. Needless to say, our condolences don't sound the same as most other people's.

I check my watch. Only one hour until visiting hours begin at the hospital. One more hour until I can sit by Magnolia's bed. Hold her hand and try not to cry in relief that she's still breathing. Her recovery is slow-moving due to the fact she broke both her legs and was unconscious for a long period of time. *She will be okay. She will be okay.*

A hand clamps on my shoulder from the back. "Hey, man. I'm glad she's going to be okay. They just told me she's going to start walking soon," Leo says, hiking his thumb to another group of SEALs. My blood begins pumping when I see Leo. It's hard to separate facts when there's so much fury flowing in my body. I'm angry mostly at myself, but Leo comes in a close motherfucking second. "I'm sorry about everything."

I swallow hard. "I don't want to get into this with you. Don't apologize."

He holds up his palms. Scared I'm going to throw a punch. Again. "I would never want to hurt them. Either of them. You have to know that." I know that.

The cause of the fire was one of the first things I asked about at the earliest opportunity.

"Could have fooled me, man. What did you think it would do to Magnolia to move in on her daughter? To break up her relationship? Both things are pretty hurtful. Although your definition of 'fucked up' might be different than mine."

"Polly asked me where you went, and I told her. I'm telling you, man. I didn't send her there. That time it wasn't malicious."

That time. This guy is such a douchebag. "Whatever, man. You're moving to Harbour Point, and I'll never have to look at your face again."

Leo shifts on his feet, uneasy, his gaze darting away.

"Out with it, prick. What else could you possibly have to say?" My tone is sharp, but I'm careful to keep the words just between us. "I have to go."

He licks his lips. "Kendall," he says, finally looking in my direction. "I, ah, really like her…as a friend."

Closing my eyes, I take a deep breath. "Are you hoping for my blessings? Because they ain't coming. Not ever. Not even when she is old enough to make those decisions on her own. Over my dead body."

"It won't be your choice soon," he says. "I am only two years older than her. You're being irrational."

I clear my throat and wonder why I didn't break his nose again when he opened his mouth. That's right. I'm at church. "There's no such thing as irrational. Only your ability to understand my rationale. I don't care about the age difference. You're a prick, and I'll never trust you."

"We're just friends, man. That's it. I wanted to see her once more before I leave for Cape Cod." Leo glances somewhere over my left shoulder, and my gaze immediately follows. Kendall is hugging the pastor and pulls back to talk to the pastor's wife.

"You're seeing her right now, aren't you? Get the fuck out of my face," I growl, rubbing my knuckles across my mouth. "Make yourself scarce, man. That goes for me and mine."

Leo grabs the back of his neck and rubs furiously. "At first I wanted to piss you off. I admit it. I saw Kendall down at the beach after you told me to stay away from Magnolia. The reason I first spoke with her was to be an ass, but I ended up enjoying…her company. Someone to talk to that wasn't someone I worked with or was trying to fuck." I step toward him, but he holds up his hand. "Just listen." I should clock him and leave him for dead, my breaths come quicker. "She talked to me and asked for advice. I gave it."

"Yeah, fucker, you told her to lie and break up a relationship. Some friend you are. You really are on the same wavelength as a kid, aren't you?"

He swallows hard. "I'm telling you it's platonic. I swear. I'm sorry for everything. Truly."

I tell him he should have found a friend his own age, someone outside of my territory, trying to be as rational and church-like as I can possibly manage to be as infuriated as I am. Leo nods as I throw him truth bombs, and he apologizes once more before I've had enough.

I take a few steps back without breaking his gaze and walk up to Kendall, putting my arm around her to guide her to the car. The conversation with Leo has me shaken. He had the ability to destroy my life once, I hope he doesn't do it again because I've pissed him off. Time is on my side. He'll be gone soon. Good riddance. If I never see that fucker again, it won't be too soon.

The ride to the hospital is crisp with the windows down. Kendall remains quiet, leaning her elbow against the open window, hanging her head halfway out. She reaches out to turn the volume down on the radio and rolls her window up. I follow suit. "Thanks for being here for me right now," she says. "This whole situation is awful, and you and Jenny are the only things that have made not having my mom bearable." It's only been a few days and several car rides to and from school. I'd do far more for her. "Especially because I was wrong about you."

I run a hand through my hair and focus on the road in front of me. "You were given wrong information. It's fine." I've dreaded this conversation. Not because I don't want to have it, but because I'm not sure how to tackle it—the appropriate thing to say or how to talk about my feelings.

"It's not. I made my own mother miserable because I thought you were going to leave," Kendall says, looking at the side of my face. "Not only did you not leave, but you also proved just how much you wanted to stay." Her voice catches. "You saved my life, Aidan. I never should have believed those things he told me." She looks forward, and I see her cross her arms on her chest. "I'll never talk to him again because of it." *Thank fuck*, I think. "I'm so used to shitty things happening that when faced with something good and honest, I don't want to believe it. She deserves it, though. My mom deserves a loyal man. I'm sorry I'm rambling on. I'm just sorry. For everything. The funeral got to me, and seeing Andrea's family twisted me in knots."

"Me too, kid. Me too. You don't have to worry about me going anywhere. I'll always be around," I say. It's a stiff promise that shocks me to the core. I won't break it, though. "I may have trips or a deployment here or there, but I'm going to stay." I turn to meet Kendall's eye, and she smiles. "Be there for you and your mom."

The smile falls quickly. "My dad will be here by now. He called and told me he wanted to visit after the fire. I told him to stay away because I didn't want to see him. Jenny said he called her and told her he was coming anyway regardless of what I want. Not really sure what to expect. Figured you might want to know." She shrugs as I pull into the parking lot.

"Are you okay with that? With seeing him? Your mom told me everything, so let me know if you want me to run interference or whatever," I reply, turning off the engine.

"It's time. We're all starting over. I feel good. Mom, though, I hope she's okay seeing him. With her." Kendall closes her eyes tightly.

"Don't worry about your mom," I say because I think it's what Magnolia would say. "Let me worry about her, okay? You focus on you." I knew going into this I was going to have to talk to Paul. This scenario probably isn't the best, and I haven't had time to think of exactly what I'd like to say to him, but Kendall is right. This is as good a time as ever. "We'll get through this."

Kendall looks appreciative as we walk into the cold, sterile building and sign in at the visitor's desk. I garner ogling looks as I'm in my uniform, but I ignore them as best I can. We get to Magnolia's room, and I'm not sure what to expect, so I set a reassuring arm on Kendall's shoulder. "You're okay, kid. You got this." I give her a pat.

She leans into the embrace as we open the door. "Thanks, Aidan. I'm sorry again," she says, looking up to meet my gaze. Amends have been made, and it feels good. It feels official. Like nothing can stand in my way. Smooth sailing from here on out.

Paul's gray gaze is scorching as I walk into the room with Kendall.

"What the hell is he doing here? In uniform to boot. Here to finish her off, soldier?" Paul snarls, looking back to the bed where Magnolia is sitting up, face flustered—and red. From crying. I twitch as his intonation grates when he calls me the wrong label. "Get over here, Kendall Sager. That guy is bad news." Paul waves, trying to get his daughter away from me. Something my childhood did prepare me for was dealing with two douchebags in the same day without breaking a sweat.

I furrow my brow. "I don't think we've had the pleasure of meeting before," I say. "Not sure I'm bad news either." The smile Magnolia loves is the one I flash at Paul.

"This is Aidan, Dad. The guy who pulled me from a flaming building," Kendall drawls, slowly, like she's talking to someone who is hard of hearing. "Nice to see you, too. Some greeting after all this time." Her grip tightens on my arm. Magnolia looks relieved to see me. Or Kendall. I don't know, and it doesn't really matter. Ignoring Paul's next insult, I walk toward the bed in the corner and take my place in the armchair.

Kendall sits on the bed and kisses Magnolia on the forehead. "I'm sorry. We left as soon as we could after the funeral. I wanted to be here before he got here. Didn't work out that way. I'm so sorry."

Magnolia scoffs, smiling. "Please, I'm a pro at dealing with your father. I'm just sorry I couldn't make Andrea's funeral." Her smirk falls and is swiftly replaced by sorrow. I lay a hand on her arm. "Paul, stop pacing," Magnolia says, exasperated. "Coming here was a mistake if you only want to argue. We don't want to. Don't have the energy to, either." The harrowing circles under Magnolia's eyes add the believability to her request.

"I didn't fight you when you wanted to move here with Kendall, Maggie. Figured it would be best for a change of scenery, but I can't accept this." He gestures to me, grimacing. "You traipsing around with all of these men, almost getting yourself killed, putting our daughter in danger." Paul stops to stand at the end of the bed. He glares at us. All three of us. A united front. He shakes his head, and anger abates to make way for pain—a displaced sense of betrayal.

Magnolia lets out a long breath that I can tell rattles her chest. "Accidents happen. We're fine. As you can clearly see. Don't be dramatic. We love our life in Bronze Bay."

"We do," Kendall chimes in. It's very obvious that seeing her father isn't comfortable. I bet she's envisioning what she walked in on. I hate that she has to bear that, but I'm glad that Paul seems to realize this fact, too. Fucking asshole. "We are happy here. Mom's going to get better, and we're going to go back to living it."

"No," Paul says, hands on hips. "You're coming back with me, Kendall. I've been too lenient. I should have forced my hand earlier. It doesn't matter what you saw or how you feel. I'm your father. You'll live half the year with me and the other half with your mother. I'll let you finish out this school year, but this summer you're moving back home."

Kendall laughs. "I'd never."

Paul glares at Magnolia. "I'll take you to court. I'll drag it out. Make it expensive and painful. You know I'm right. The girl needs her father."

Her face wilts. "One, I have more money than you. Two, you'd really do that to us? Knowing it's not what she wants? She'll be eighteen soon, Paul. Remember? It's not even worth the effort. She's not a little girl who wants to stand on your shoes while dancing in the living room. Those days are gone. I don't want to fight you, but I'd think after all these years you'd have the decency to respect my role as a mother. I'll always do what is best for her."

"You're in a hospital bed, Magnolia. Who is caring for her?"

Kendall stands. "No one needs to take care of me, but if you must know, Aidan and Jenny have been helping out since I left the hospital. I'm not moving in with you, Dad. You won't take Mom to court, either. I'll tell them every gory detail. I'll spread that story like gospel. No judge would put me back in your house for any length of time knowing how much it would damage me emotionally. I thought you came here to make amends. You're still the same selfish person you've always been. Where is the other woman?" Kendall sneers, bringing that catty teenager out to play. I cringe.

"I need to talk to my family," Paul says, directing the statement to me. "Alone."

Magnolia shakes her hand, putting her hand on my

arm. "He's staying. Anything you have to say to us you can say in front of Aidan."

"Seriously, Maggie?"

I clear my throat. I've sat silent long enough. Paul isn't an opponent in any sense. His salt-and-pepper hair is long and shaggy, and he's long and lean. I could dispatch of him so quickly I'd be considered a lethal weapon in a court of law. Instead, I say, "Magnolia is serious." Had she wanted privacy in this fucked-up family moment, I would have respected it. Could even understand it a bit. They were an established unit far before I came into the picture. "It's probably best if you go."

"Fuck you, man. Get out of here. These are my girls," Paul says, eyes glinting with challenge.

That's all it takes. I didn't fight hard enough for them in the past, but it's obvious this is where I'm supposed to be. My fight.

I stand up to my full height and take two steps toward Paul. He wobbles as he tries to step away from my looming presence. "These aren't your girls. Not after what you did. You lost them a long time ago. This is what happens when men do bad things, Paul. Good men swoop in and steal the things they used to care about. These are my girls now. I care about them. I love them. I would die for them. I almost did. I will fight for them and with them until I take my very last breath. Magnolia is wild and beautiful—the special kind of beautiful, because when I met her, she had no idea of her worth. I did, though. I saw every scar and every memory she shared with me as my chance. As the wrapping paper of a gift I've waited my whole life for."

Paul takes another shaky step backward. I step

forward in time with his backward movement. I nod at him. "You will let Kendall stay where she wants. You won't give Magnolia any more grief because she doesn't deserve that. No," I say, choking on my words. "Because she's good, Paul. Not like you."

"You can't just steal my family," Paul hisses, gaze darting anywhere except my face. "That's not how it works."

Instead of threatening him further, I back up toward Magnolia's bed. "It is exactly how this works. But you are right, I can't just steal them. I didn't have to steal them, Paul. You gave them to me. They're pretty awesome. Thanks for that, by the way."

"Fuck you!" Paul screeches, waving his middle finger in my direction like a deranged lunatic. He stutters, "Maggie, please. I need to talk to you."

"He's right," Magnolia says, chiming in. "You lost me a long time ago, but Kendall can visit you if she wants and if her psychologist thinks it's a good idea, but we aren't your girls anymore."

Magnolia squeezes my hand. When I look at her big blue eyes, I see gratitude and love. We haven't discussed anything pertaining to our relationship while she's been in the hospital. I told her to focus all of her energy on getting better. This is the first time hope blossoms in my chest. In this heated, uncomfortable moment, I become aware that we don't just look like family, we might actually be one. Formed of heartbreak. Of betrayal. Joined because of circumstances and forged by the choice of love.

I don't kiss her to put on a show for Paul. I kiss her to tell her that I understand what she's telling me by not saying anything at all. It's gentle. Just her lips glazed in tears and my own with desperate relief in this confirmation. Neither of us closes our eyes. They stay locked for the brief kiss. I pull away when I hear Kendall say, "If you had come in here and asked me what I wanted, I might have said I'd like to start spending time with you again. You went about this the wrong way. We're getting over a trauma, and you're heaping more awful on the plate. Dad, please just go home to Pamela. I'll call you. I promise."

Paul isn't looking at Kendall. He's staring at Magnolia, who is staring at me. My heart lurches at the scene. This is the moment when he finally feels the loss. Realizes what he gave up for selfish pleasure.

"Let me ask you something, Paul," I bark.

He shakes his head while wearing a sardonic smile. "What?"

"Were you afraid?"

"Afraid of what?"

"Of losing them? When you were carrying on the affair, did it occur to you that you may lose Magnolia…Kendall, because of it? What does that kind of fear feel like?"

His face falls, and he nods at Magnolia, then at his daughter. "You tell me," he fires back.

I quirk one brow.

"You've obviously felt that kind of fear. You're feeling it now that I'm here trying to win them back."

"Win them back?" Magnolia asks, voice loud. "Paul, please." Kendall excuses herself in the guise of taking a phone call, but I know she's feeling conflicted and uncomfortable, her tense body language says a lot.

After the door closes, Paul replies, "Yeah, Maggie. Doesn't matter though, does it? You're so over me, you've replaced me."

"Is this the point where I'm supposed to feel sorry

for you? That you cheated on me? Forgive me for being confused."

He hangs his head, and I'd like to disappear into the hallway. "Pamela left. She was cheating with some kid, and I kicked her out." The whole story follows, and by the time he finishes talking about the wedding cancellations and the return of all the wedding gifts and the spray paint on his car and side of his house, I almost feel bad for him. Magnolia is eating it up, the ultimate karma. Paul tells us he's checked into the local hotel and will leave tomorrow, and when it's finally time for Magnolia to respond to him, she wishes him a good day and shakes her head.

"Your affair is the reason I found true love, Paul. I won't say I'm grateful for what I went through, because Kendall came along for the ride, but I'm grateful for the gift I was given because of it. Aidan is good for me. For us."

"Yeah, yeah. Don't have to rub it in. I gotta go. Nice to share my life story with a stranger," Paul says, meeting my gaze. "As always, good to see you, Maggie. I hope you get better soon."

Magnolia sniffles and confirms she's set for release soon. After Paul leaves, closing the door, I sit next to her in the bed. She looks up at me, and I smile at her. Simplicity at its finest after an hour of unrelenting drama.

"That smile of yours. If I were sitting on a stool, I'd be falling on the floor right now," she says, biting her bottom lip.

"If you were falling, I'd be catching. And looking at your black lace panties."

"Spoiler alert, I'm not wearing panties. Hospitals force nude sexiness or mesh grandma panties."

Taking her face in my hand, I bring my lips to hers again. "I don't care what you have on, I'm just glad you're mine. I meant what I said," I say, mouth moving against her lips. "I want you forever."

"I like that idea," Magnolia says, wincing in pain when she tries to move her legs to change position to be closer to me. "Though it might be a while until you can unwrap your gift."

"Good thing I'm patient."

Magnolia pecks the tip of my nose. "Thanks for that. For standing up for us. For Kendall. Those things you said mean a lot to me, and I know they mean a lot to her. Paul will come around. He's not good with change."

He's not good at a lot of things, and who the hell is good with change? Some people can pretend better than others. Paul can take his threats and his bad decisions and leave Magnolia alone. "Don't thank me. This is us now. I'd do far more for you. I love you, Magnolia."

"I'm glad you're a thief," she chirps. "I love you too, Aidan Mixx."

She lays her hand on my chest, right in the center.

EIGHTEEN

Magnolia

Healing is a bitch. Recovery is slow-moving, and my desire to get up and go implodes on me most days. Aidan set up a bed for me in the downstairs living room, and I usually sit down on it at the end of the day, wincing in pain. Two compound fractures in each leg at different points. Three surgeries and about twelve red jagged scars later, I'm able to walk without the use of crutches or a walker. I still use a cane, as one side needs a little more help than the other. Kendall decorated it in her school colors, all glitter and strips of cloth, and deemed it a "swaggy cane." I'm ready to return back to my life before. I miss the auctions and spending all day working on refinishing a piece without having to take a break.

The pain is something I can deal with because it only affects me. I can grin and bear anything life throws my way. The emotions that barrage when I think of the night of the fire are something else altogether. That breed of pain is inescapable, and no matter how many times I'm told that Andrea died in honor, doing what she was called to do, the guilt doesn't ease. It's a miracle I'm alive—that Kendall and Aidan made it out. It sure puts life in perspective when you almost bite the big one. It's something I work at every day. Forgiving myself. Moving on. Being appreciative of the gift of life she gave while still honoring her sacrifice.

Kendall's eighteenth birthday passed, and I bought her a car. Well, Aidan and Jenny helped locate something reliable, and I footed the bill. Now she's driving all of the time. If a parenting manual did exist, I'm sure there would be a whole chapter devoted to the fear you feel watching your child drive away into the big, bad world surrounded by people who haven't been vetted. Her independence is something she's longed for —craved. No longer a child with a woman's mind. She was forced to grow up and realize life's hard truths before most of her peers. Initially I thought it wasn't a good thing. Who wants their child to grow up too fast? But maybe this hiccup in our life will provide a solid foundation, something to learn from.

The front door slams as she runs into the living room, backpack slung over one shoulder. "Hey, Mom. Today's the day, right? You're moving upstairs to your room again? Are you sure you're ready?"

"Yes," I nearly shout. Laughing, I clear my throat. "I'm sorry. That was loud and obnoxious. I want my life back. This house is great and all, but I haven't been out of our yard except for doctor's appointments for weeks. Moving to my room is another step toward freedom. Upstairs today, and the sky is the limit next week."

"It's not that bad," Kendall replies, redistributing the weight of her pack to the other shoulder. "You could be at Dad's house recovering." She laughs. It's a little bit awful that she jokes like that, but I'm loosening my fists, letting her find her own self, and she's doing a damn fine job. "Is Aidan coming for dinner?" she asks. He's over almost every day after work. When he's not, Jenny is here annoying me with Bronze Bay gossip and asking me if I'm finished being a princess because she's bored and doesn't have anyone to go out with.

"Did you call your father back?" I ask. "Aidan texted a bit ago, and he was running behind. Not sure if he'll make it home for dinner."

She rolls her eyes. "I did call him. He asked if I wanted to spend a couple weeks with him this summer. I told him I'd think about it. I have cheer camp and stuff with Juliet." Progress.

I dip my head. "I think it's a good idea. He's trying. He's lonely, too."

My daughter shakes a finger at me. "Don't feel bad for him. He dug his lonely grave, Mom. I shouldn't have to remind you. Oh, did he say anything about dessert then? If he wasn't going to be on time for dinner?" Kendall asks, her blue eyes sliding to the window behind me.

"Who? Aidan? Why would he say anything about dessert? Why are you acting weird?" We're finally at a point when I don't have to defend myself against Paul or the memories. They don't get trapped in my mind anymore. The chapter of that book is closed. I've started something brand new. Or I'm trying to if my legs would cooperate. I snap in front of Kendall's face to draw her attention. "Earth to Kendall." I open my eyes wide and find her gaze.

"Sorry. Sorry. Thought I saw something outside for a second. Just a bird or squirrel, never mind. I have homework to do." Juliet bustles in the door on the phone with someone, talking far louder than she needs to. Kendall sighs and says, "She was outside fighting with her boyfriend. I had to listen to that all the way home from school." She scoffs and calls out to her friend, "Hang up, Juliet. We have homework! You're fighting in circles. Wasting everyone's time!"

Juliet hangs up the call, and the girls tromp upstairs, Kendall inciting a single girl's mantra as she lectures her friend. I grin. She'll never take crap from a man. Not even a little.

Grabbing the pile of sheets from this godforsaken bed, I head toward the laundry room, doing my best walk-hobble with the cane. A buzzer sounds in the kitchen, and I make my way to check on the chicken. Being relinquished to the house has made me a better chef over the past few months. I turn off the oven and move to the freezer to see if we have any ice cream for dessert.

My phone chimes with a text in my back pocket. It's from Aidan.

Tell Kendall dinner is ready and come outside.

I stare at the message, then look out the window. I can't see the driveway in the front, and I'm not fast enough at the moment to check. I tap back,

Okay. Everything okay?

His reply bubbles back.

Perfect

I tilt my head to the side and shake it. "Why are they being so weird?" I whisper to myself. I don't have to tell Kendall dinner is ready. She and Juliet are coming downstairs and are in the kitchen in the next second. Kendall grabs the potholders and pulls the chicken out of the oven.

"Aidan is outside, Mom. We can serve ourselves. Lots of homework anyway." Juliet waves a thick textbook to make her point. "I'll leave a plate for you." Kendall smiles so wide, it makes me smile.

"Are you guys okay?" I shake my head.

She nods, a wistful look in her eye. "Go, Mom."

Aidan calls out from the mudroom, his head appearing from above the swinging doors. "It was sort of an asshole move to ask you to come outside. Let me help you," he says, hazel gaze shifting between me and Kendall. Aidan is in his uniform. Full whites, his cover clutched in his hand. I lose my breath.

He walks over, winks at Kendall, and links his arm in mine. "You feeling okay today? Okay enough to get out of here for a little while?"

"Of course I'm okay to get out of here. You are all acting like madmen! Where are we going? Why can't we eat dinner with the girls? You're so fancy, and I'm wearing jeans and a sweatshirt." I lift the slouchy pink material and let it fall. "Do I have time to change?"

Aidan turns to face me. "You look beautiful, Magnolia. Perfect." Leaning forward, he takes a section of hair and winds it around his fingers. He presses a soft kiss against my mouth and pulls away too soon.

The girls catcall from behind us. My stomach flips. Every single time he touches me. The anticipation is wild after months of being separated by injury. We both decided it would be best to wait until my recovery in a more stable place before we attacked each other with our clothes off. Me moving up to my room today means more than just switching beds. "Let's go," Aidan says, smiling.

"Stay home. Do your homework," I say, unable to hide my red cheeks from Kendall.

Kendall smirks. "I'm spending the night at Juliet's tonight. We came here to eat dinner because you cook better than Ms. Jenny. Hope that's okay."

I'm about to argue, it's a school night, but then I remember Aidan's lips against mine. "Jenny knows?"

Juliet grins. "She knows."

"Okay then. Drive safe and text me when you get there."

Aidan wraps an arm around my waist and waves his free hand at them. "Be good," he says.

"Be good?" I say once we're out of earshot. "That's like telling them to open a meth lab and get pregnant with twins. You have so much to learn," I say, shaking my head.

"Next time should I say, 'be bad and do whatever you want'?" Aidan asks, helping me into the car and arranging my cane in the back seat.

"Probably," I say, sighing. "Are you going to tell me what's going on? Where are we going?"

Turning out of the drive, he heads for the main road that leads to downtown. His smile is palpable. "There's something I want to show you, that's all."

"You're so excited. I hope when I see this, I offer the proper amount of excitement," I tease, laying a hand on his leg. He flinches a little. We've avoided physical contact for too long. "Can we make plans for later on tonight?"

"Magnolia, you're killing me. We start talking about tonight, and I'll pull the car over right now. We both know your crippled status isn't conducive to back-seat fucking." A wave of desire hits me as the crude images come to mind.

"You're right," I agree.

Aidan laughs. "Glad we're on the same page. I'm going to need you to put this on," he says, handing me a black blindfold he pulled from under his leg.

"You just said we weren't having car sex. Why are you throwing sex toys in my lap?" I say, stretching the mask over my face.

He growls. "Okay, one-track mind. I need you blind so I can surprise you."

"Fine. But if you wanted to touch me, I'd be okay with that as well."

"You will be the death of me, woman."

"Don't die. I need your dick tonight," I counter, smiling so wide my cheeks hurt.

"You're relentless," he replies, making a turn. I can feel when he puts the car into park.

"And it's been a really long time since you've touched me," I say, knowing his hands aren't busy now that the vehicle isn't moving.

His hands touch my face. My whole body prickles. Aidan runs his fingers across my jaw and turns my face to the side. When my lips meet his, the electricity kicks into overdrive. It's the first kiss we've shared in months that has the passion to tell me we'll move past second base. His tongue is languid as he relishes the connection. Just as my hands reach out for him, he ends the kiss.

I lick my lips, tasting him. "More," I say, making a move to remove the blindfold. "I want to see you."

"Keep it on just a little while longer. And as for more, I'll give you all that you want later tonight. Stay put, I'm going to open the door for you." I hear him tap out a text and send it. I'm hyperaware being blinded. The car door opening and closing seems loud, and my own breaths resemble a gusting wind I can't control. The passenger-side door opens, and his hands are helping me up.

"Blinding a cripple is probably not legal. Can you please let me take off this mask before you make me walk?"

Aidan helps just enough to let me walk on my own without my cane. "Ten more seconds," he says, forcing us forward a few more steps. "I want to see your face." His tone is low. If I could confirm by sight, I'd say he was nervous.

He removes the blindfold, and like I suspected, we are in the downtown area of Bronze Bay. Maybe it's because I haven't been here for a while, but more than likely this building has had so much work done, it takes me a full five seconds to realize what I'm looking at. This house has always been decrepit and old. The realtors said whoever bought the land would tear down the structure and build something new.

I tear my gaze from the beautiful, completely remodeled Victorian-style house to meet Aidan's gaze. He's staring at me, biting his lip, a bead of sweat sliding down the side of his face.

"Do you like it? I know it's not the same as Magnolia's Steals, but I matched the shade of paint, and it looks amazing inside," he explains, gesturing with his free hand, the one that isn't wrapped around me for support. "It's pretty much empty because, as you know, everything was a loss at the old store, but I went to a couple of auctions and bought a few things. You know, I thought maybe I could pick some stuff out that you'd like to sell. Things I saw in the store before or packaged for shipping. It's probably all wrong, I know. I wanted you to have something to come back to. I worked with the insurance adjusters and handled everything for you. There's nothing to worry about, Magnolia. This is yours, and if you hate it and you're mad that I didn't consult with you, I understand completely." He's shaking. Aidan's whole body is vibrating—waiting for my assessment.

Tears spring to my eyes as my gaze lands on the storefront window. He draws my attention back to his face. "This is the nicest thing anyone has ever done for me. It's perfect, Aidan. I can't believe you went through all this trouble. It's stunning." I laugh a short burst. "I love it more than I loved the old store. How is that possible? This is too much." Suddenly I'm struck with how large of a gesture this is, and my heart aches.

His hazel gaze is wide. "Magnolia," he says, choking up. "It will never be enough. I'll never be able to do enough for you. Not in one lifetime."

I sniffle, and he guides me closer to the window, the one that he definitely had put in because the old house didn't have a window this big and this beautiful. There is a display set up, I now realize. It resembles the scene I set up for Christmas, and my stomach sinks. The fire. The reminder. I close my eyes and blink away several tears. It's different, though. It has little houses lining a street that resembles the downtown in Bronze Bay. In front of the purple house is figurines of a man on his knee extending a ring box, and the woman is standing, both hands clasped against her chest. My breathing quickens when I recognize what's happening in the display. I'm so intent on focusing on every other detail that I lean forward to put both hands on the window.

Slowly, I turn my head and find Aidan kneeling on the sidewalk, ring box extending up to me. "Hi, I'm Aidan Mixx," he says, words shaky, hand trembling.

I know this game. Through tears, I say, "Hi, I'm Magnolia Sager. It's nice to meet you." He grins.

"Reset button?" Aidan asks, his questioning eyes full of hope. He removes the sparkling diamond from the box and turns his palm up, requesting my left hand. I give it to him.

"Reset," I reply as he slides the ring on my finger. He looks so dashing and handsome. The picture of love and respect. He stands, taking me in his arms. Seeking out his lips, I kiss him deeply.

Clapping starts mid-kiss. I turn in his arms to see a crowd of people smiling wide and cheering. Jenny is in there, and so are Kendall and Juliet. Andrea's family looks tearful as they witness Aidan's act of selfless love and the proposal. Everyone who means something to us is here for this moment. All of Aidan's cohorts are in uniform, fists in the air. An older woman breaks off from the crowd and walks toward us.

Aidan squeezes me once. Then I realize who it is. It's his mother. She visited me once in the hospital, but it was when I first arrived, so the meeting was very foggy. Her smile reminds me of Aidan's, and I feel the sharp pang of sympathy for Aidan. "Mrs. Mixx," I say, slipping from Aidan's tight hold. "It's so nice to see you."

She shakes her head. "No, seeing you two is nice. Thank you for letting me be here to see this, son."

Aidan swallows hard, running a hand through his hair. "I moved my mom here," he says, meeting my gaze. "It wasn't permanent when I first brought her over, but she's happy here, and I think it will be a good thing."

I open my eyes, shocked. "A good thing? It's a great thing. An amazing thing. I'm so happy for you," I say, locking eyes with Mrs. Mixx. "For both of you." Aidan told me he visited her and that things were choppy but improving. I didn't push the boundaries by asking for details, but I'm so proud of him. For overcoming. For being the man I always knew he could be, and by doing the world's hardest act: forgiving.

"Sometimes all we need is the grace of a reset button," she says, squeezing her son's arm, then meeting my gaze. "It's the greatest gift of my life."

Aidan's tearful gaze is soft as he leans over to hug her, and my heart swells. Mrs. Mixx pushes away. "You two enjoy this moment. I love you. The both of you."

When she returns to the crowd, I'm visibly shaken with emotion. Aidan brushes the tears from under my eyes. "That was a yes, right?"

I nod. "A forever yes," I confirm. "This was so beautiful, Aidan. All of it. Thank you so much for this."

He brushes his lips softly against mine. "Thank you for giving me a life."

Wiping my nose and hiccupping, I laugh. "You're welcome. Now, I think there's something else you're supposed to give me tonight."

He pulls away, a glimmer of feral desire spiking. "Only one thing?"

Epilogue

AIDAN

SHE'S SILHOUETTED against the window, her curves on display as she looks over the ocean. Magnolia is naked, ready, and most importantly, she's my wife. To have and to hold. For the rest of my life. Approaching her, I drop a kiss on her shoulder, and she turns to look at me, finding my lips with her own. It's the last night in my apartment before I move in with her. She's made a big bed on the floor like the first time we spent the night together, and I'm looking forward to having her body any which way she'll give it to me.

"You tired?" I ask.

She helped me move the rest of my stuff into her house today.

She quirks one brow. "What do you think?" she replies, reaching a soft hand out to trail down my chest and abs, and ends on my cock. "I mean, if you're tired. I get it. You were moving all those heavy boxes."

My body reacts instantly to her touch, hardening to my full length and girth. "Magnolia, I could have performed far more energy-draining activities, and I'd still want to fuck you all night. Let's be honest with each other." My fingers trail between her legs to find her soft and wet. Dipping a finger in, I watch as her eyes close and her head falls against my chest.

I laugh at the instantaneous reaction. "Don't laugh. It's not funny." Magnolia pants.

"It's kind of funny. It's a good thing."

"It's why I have your rings on my finger," Magnolia retorts, yelping in pleasure as I press against her G-spot and rub back and forth. "That feels so good."

I pull out of her, and she shudders in frustration. "You only married me because I'm good with my hands?" I say, mock hurt on my face, brow furrowed. She smirks, takes my dick in her hand and kneels to put it in her mouth. It's my turn to groan as I watch her slide it in and out of her mouth, licking a long line from base to tip every few pumps. "Go ahead, you're going to work me into a frenzy and then stop abruptly, right? I'm on to you."

She smiles around my cock, and I think I might come right then and there. "You really are going to kill me, Magnolia."

She pops her lips off of me and stands. Running a finger along my lip, she says, "I don't want to do that, now do I? I want you forever, and you're wrong. I'm not going to work you into a frenzy and then stop. I'm going to work you into a frenzy and then sink down onto your cock and ride you." With her pointer finger that might as well be a fist, she pushes my chest.

Backing up to the pallet of blankets on the floor, I lie down and fold my arms behind my head.

She's a vision of sexual prowess and beauty as she stalks toward me and follows me down. Her lips are everywhere, and finally, she brings her sweet pussy right where we both want it. Riding me up and down at an infuriatingly slow pace, she brings herself to the brink of orgasm. Every muscle in my body is coiled, ready to release, but I hold back until she comes. I hold back because I want to remember this moment. The one where my wife takes her pleasure from my body while simultaneously giving me the world.

Magnolia sinks all the way down until she's filled herself with me. I grit my teeth as I feel her cunt grip my cock as she explodes into orgasm. She doesn't have to ride me anymore. Feeling her wrap around me as love-laced moans ricochet off the walls of my empty apartment is all it takes for me. I grab her hips to hold her in place and release deep inside her. Collapsing on my chest, I can taste her breaths as she pants in relief.

"Round one," I say, kissing her ear.

She kisses me, holding my face. I'm in for it. I can see it in her face. "Will you go down on me next, and then you can be on top? Also, from behind, in front of that window, and then more of your tongue between my legs?"

My softening hard-on immediately responds to her request. I laugh. "You have quite the itinerary." I jut my hips up, and she moans. My cock reports to steel-hard status. "Are you sure you want me to pull out to go down on you?"

"No. You're right," she says, closing her eyes, pulling at my shoulders to roll me on top of her without disconnecting our bodies. "Aidan Mixx, I love you so much."

"Not because I'm inside you?" I reply, biting my lip.

She shakes her head left and right, her eyes still closed as she languidly appreciates my thrusts. Her lashes flutter as her gaze finds mine. Laying a hand on my cheek, she says, "Because you're mine."

My heart does that thing. Where it beats and stops at the same time. "I love you too."

Bad boys don't reform. There isn't some lesson we learn that turns the tides. What happens, and I'm pretty sure it's true for most of us, is that we casually stumble into the woman made for only us. Sometimes it's not lightning striking or a divine symbol reflecting a "This Is It!" sign above their heads. It's in the way they praise you. Touch you a little differently than all those who came before. It's in the way they react to your smile. How they live without you. When you tally the score, it's undeniable proof that what you're feeling is real. There is no hesitation in requiring more of their love. Their time. Their life. There's no doubt there is only one.

Kendall graduates on a Tuesday and leaves for college the following Friday. She was accepted into a summer study program that lets her start her freshman year early. The air is hot, and the breeze is strong as I close the trunk on Kendall's car. Magnolia is a mess—crying off and on constantly. She's standing next to me, clasping my hand so tightly I've lost all blood flow to my right arm.

"I left my phone charger in the house," Kendall says, jogging up the front steps to go in the house.

Magnolia sniffs and whispers, "Only a few more minutes. I only have to hold it together for a few more minutes."

I'd be lying if I said I wasn't choked up a bit, too. If not because the emotions rolling off Magnolia are intense, but because I'll miss the kid myself, too. My mom comes out on the porch and slowly makes her way down the steps. She's happy here, becoming accustomed to the slow, beachy way of life this small town offers. She has bingo at the fire station every Friday and gin with the girls that work at the general store on Wednesday nights. Starting over with my mother hasn't been all peaches and cream. I have questions about my childhood, and she has answers. Sometimes not ones I want to hear, but she always gives me honesty, and that's all I can ask for. We're repairing our bond one day at a time.

The woman standing next to me was the one to stir that milestone, and I'll be forever grateful for the push in the right direction. Kendall kisses my mom on the cheek. "Bye, Mimi. Keep these two out of trouble. I'm sure now that I'm out of the house they're going to rage and party. Keep them cool," she says, smirking at me. "Make sure they don't do anything stupid."

My mom laughs, a throaty cackle I never remember hearing during my youth. It's a new memory. One I'm fond of. "They'll rage. And they'll miss you with all their heart, darling. Go get that degree. Stay away from the boys. Always wear clean underpants, and tell the truth even if you lose friends for it."

I nod, running a hand over my mouth. Sound advice. "Yes. Stay away from boys," I echo one sentiment.

Kendall laughs. "Come on, Aidan. I'm an adult now." She waggles her brows.

Magnolia sighs next to me, trying her best to stay

strong. "Boston is so far away, honey." This was a point of contention. It's where Kendall dreamed of going. It's far away from Florida, and the time she'll be able to visit home will be scarce. "Call me every day. Even twice a day if you feel like it. If you ever need anything, just ask. I'll be right there."

"We'll both be there if you need us," I add. "Now drive safe and get out of here before your poor mom loses her mind."

Magnolia hits my shoulder playfully and pulls her daughter into her arms. The hug lasts a long time, and neither of them is ready for it to end. A tear slips down Kendall's face, and she's quick about brushing it away.

She meets my eyes, and her grin widens. Mouthing the words "Thank you," she pulls away from the embrace and walks toward me. "Give me some good advice," she says, standing taller than she was moments before. "A big ole SEAL like you must have something really intuitive and insightful for me before I go off into the world outside of Bronze Bay."

Magnolia cries out when she's reminded that Kendall is leaving even though the car is packed to the nines and the engine is on and waiting. She covers her mouth and reins it in. "This is harder than I thought it would be. I'm sorry." Magnolia moves back to link arms with my mom and leans her head on her shoulder as she wipes at her face with a disintegrating tissue.

Under my breath, I say, "Well first, never forget how much that woman loves you," I tease.

Kendall smiles, shaking her head. "Like I could forget." I can see the emotion swelling in her eyes. "What else?"

I nod once, meet Magnolia's eyes, and look back to

my stepdaughter. "Not everyone gets a reset button, Kendall. Don't be afraid to live full throttle." I shake my head, placing a hand on her shoulder. "Cherish the moments you're happy. Learn from the ones when you're sad, and whatever you do, never let your past cloud your present."

She leans in and hugs me. "I won't," Kendall promises. When she releases me, she kisses Magnolia once more, and she's gone.

"Come on inside, I made lunch," Mom says, leaving us to return to the kitchen. I affirm we'll be inside in a second and take Magnolia into my arms.

"I'm going to miss her so much," she says.

"She's going to miss you," I reply.

Magnolia kisses me, snot smearing under my nose. She apologizes when she pulls away and uses her wadded tissue to wipe it off me. I cringe. "You going to pull it together so we can try out our new bed tonight?" It's her newest auction purchase.

"Of course," she cries out. "I'll never miss a chance to *sleep* with you."

Pressing my lips together, I raise one brow. "Mrs. Mixx, I don't want to sleep with you."

She pretends to be offended.

"I want to put a baby inside you."

Magnolia blushes a furious shade of red. "And start all over?" she says.

Cupping her cheek, I kiss her softly once. "Reset."

Author's note

I've never written a book about a mother before. I think it's because the task always seemed too large, too powerful. To encapsulate and effectively portray a role that means so much to so many people. My mom raised me by herself. Granted, my dad was in the picture and helped out a lot, and I had grandparents that loved me dearly, I think, for a daughter, it's their mother that dictates the strong character traits they embody. Some may say that coming from a divorced home is a negative, that it weakens the children, but I'm living proof that the broken home I came from, as do so many others, had a positive impact in my life well into adulthood. I knew early on what hard work and sacrifice looked like. I saw firsthand how difficult it was for my mom to be at a million different places at the same time and still get dinner on the table.

She is a hero. A living, breathing representation of how you take a bad decision, or a difficult time and you use it to shape yourself and your children. Her resiliency prepared me to be a military wife. Her fierce determination is why I will never quit something I start. Her work ethic is to be admired by all. Her honesty in the face of adversity is a testament to the person she is and now to the person she raised.

I tilt my hat to the single mothers out there. No one deserves respect and admiration like you do. I hope you know how much you're loved. They're watching. Give them something fierce and brave to look at.

A Look At: The Forgotten SEAL

THE REAL SEAL BOOK ONE

Two shattered souls. One unexpected chance at healing.

Carina Painter has it all—on paper. A bestselling author with a carefully curated life, she hides the truth behind her smile: a childhood of chaos and an engagement that left emotional wounds she can't outrun. When a chance meeting offers her an escape, she grabs it—desperate for something real.

Smith Eppington, a Navy SEAL scarred by war and a tragic accident, is a man haunted by memories he can't fully recall. With most of his body marked and his best friend lost, he's given up on finding peace—until Carina enters his world, pen in hand and curiosity burning.

What starts as an interview quickly turns into something deeper: a connection born from pain, resilience, and the possibility of something more. But as Carina helps Smith unearth the truth about his past, the answers they find may cost them the fragile hope they've built.

Can love rewrite the story of their lives—or will the truth end their final chapter before it begins?

AVAILABLE NOW

Rachel grew up in a small, quiet town full of loud talkers. Her words were always only loud on paper. She has been writing stories and creating characters for as long as she can remember. CRAZY GOOD and SET IN STONE, and TIME AND SPACE, three of her Navy SEAL novels are INTERNATIONAL BESTSELLERS. After living in San Diego, Virginia Beach, and then Fairfax, VA, she now resides in colorful Colorado with her badass husband, two children, her Sphynx cat, & her dog, Polly.

www.racheljrobinson.com
Rachel Robinson's Racy Readers